AUDREY ORR

and the

ROBOT RAGE

Audrey Orr and the Robot Rage
An original concept by author Jenny Moore
© Jenny Moore

Cover artwork by Ipek Konak

Published by MAVERICK ARTS PUBLISHING LTD
Studio 11, City Business Centre, 6 Brighton Road,
Horsham, West Sussex, RH13 5BB
+44 (0) 1403 256941
© Maverick Arts Publishing Limited March 2020

A CIP catalogue record for this book is available
at the British Library.

ISBN: 978-1-84886-636-2

AUDREY ORR
and the
ROBOT RAGE

JENNY MOORE

For Daniel, Lucy and Dafydd, with love

1

Strictly Mum Dancing

Audrey Orr's mum was one of life's winners—and she finally had the letter to prove it.

"I won!" she shrieked, grabbing Audrey by the shoulders and dancing her across the kitchen.

"I won!" she screamed, grabbing Mr Orr by the waist and prancing him round the dining table.

"I won!" she squealed, grabbing poor old Mr Windybags by the scruff of his neck and thrusting him into the air like a winner's trophy. She put him down again pretty quickly, after Mr Windybags did what Mr Windybags did best, but Audrey guessed it would take more than a farty cat to dampen her mum's spirits. After ten years of entering competitions, with nothing more exciting to show for her efforts than a pair of men's golfing socks (which seemed to come with a free fungal foot infection), Mrs Orr had never looked happier. "I won! I won! I won!"

"Yes. So we gathered," said Mr Orr, scratching at his manky mushroom foot with the blunt end of a fork. Those golfing socks had a lot to answer for. "Come on, Kat, are you going to tell us *what* you've won or do we have to guess?"

Audrey hoped it was a new car. One with blacked-out windows, so no one could see her stupid eye patch or Grandad's woolly car accessories. Turning up to her old school in Mum's rusty orange banger had been embarrassing enough. But it was a hundred times worse since they'd moved to Ivy Ridge and Grandad had discovered the unlikely joys of knitting. The 'Katmobile' now sported stripy woollen seat covers, a lumpy yellow aerial warmer, and a giant knitted slug dangling down from the front mirror. It looked like something Mr Windybags might have coughed up in someone's slipper after eating too much grass.

"It's…" said Mrs Orr, flapping the letter around like a flag. "It's… Oh my goodness. You're not going to believe it."

Perhaps it's a really big new car, thought Audrey. *Something long and shiny, with expensive bum-warming leather seats. Or a caravan. Or a house.*

"It's a holiday," said Mrs Orr, breathless with excitement. "To Norway! I've *always* wanted to go there…" She did a celebratory leap past the fridge. "Norway," she said again. "Home of IKEA and ABBA and Swedish meatballs…"

"Er, I think you'll find that's Sweden, Mum," Audrey pointed out.

Judging by the dreamy look in her eyes, Mrs Orr wasn't going to let a bit of geography spoil the moment. "Close enough," she trilled, leaping on past the so-called biscuit cupboard. There were never any proper biscuits in there—just those horrid cardboard oat things from the health food shop and Dad's fungal foot cream collection, which was too big to fit in the medicine box. It was also the cupboard where Audrey kept her spare eye patches. So more like a Cupboard of Doom really.

"I'm sure they have meatballs in Norway as well," said Mrs Orr. "And flat-pack furniture. Not that we'll need any of that on our luxury winners' cruise!"

And with that she was off again, waltzing Audrey round and round the kitchen like an embarrassing contestant on *Strictly Mum Dancing*.

But for once Audrey didn't care. She didn't care when she bumped her hip for the tenth time that day (it was tricky judging distances with only one eye on the job). She didn't care when she caught sight of her reflection in the oven door, with the horrible pink and silver eye patch over her glasses that made her look like a disco pirate. She didn't care about anything. *A cruise*, she thought, grinning dizzily to herself as they picked up speed. *I'm going on a cruise to Norway!*

"A cruise?" repeated Mr Orr. "On a boat, you mean? On water?" He frowned. "Don't you remember the *last* time we tried that?"

Audrey—and most of the other passengers, she imagined—had been trying to forget the family's fateful trip to the Scilly Isles last summer. Mr Orr never did find his sea legs. But he found his sea stomach alright, emptying it all over an entire row of holidaymakers. Twice.

"Oh, Pooh-pooh," said Mrs Orr. Not because she thought it was a silly thing to say, but because that was her pet name for her husband. Everyone else called him 'Paul' or 'Dad' or 'Mr Orr'. But to Audrey's mum—and to Audrey's red-cheeked shame—he'd always be her 'Pooh-pooh': *Hurry up, Pooh-pooh, it's dinner time... Mr Windybags has left you a little present in your slipper, Pooh-pooh... Watch out for that steaming dog poo, Pooh-pooh...*

"Don't worry. You'll be fine," Mrs Orr promised her husband as she twirled. "The ship's so enormous you won't feel it bobbing up and down at all. It's like a floating hotel. And it says here you can eat and drink as much as you like. *Everything's* included! They've even got a Soft-Scoop-2000!"

"What's a Soft-Scoop-2000?" asked Audrey.

"Who cares?" said her dad, who'd perked up considerably at the mention of complimentary food. "It's free—that's all that matters!" And with that, he danced round the kitchen after them, singing:

"Happy free food to me,

Happy free food to me,

Happy free food in my tum-my,

Happy free food to me."

Mr Orr's singing was nearly as embarrassing as Mrs Orr's silly nicknames. But nothing could keep the grin off Audrey's face now. In her mind's eye, she was already sailing up the magnificent fjords from her National Geographic calendar, with beautiful mountains on either side and a chilled lemonade in her hand. She was already exploring new towns and cities to use in her secret comic strip, *Orz Um's Awesome Adventures*.

Orz was everything Audrey wasn't: brave, popular and super pretty. That's because Orz didn't have to wear sticky plastic patches over one side of her glasses, like a lopsided freak. She didn't have a laz-*y* left eye, like Audrey, she had a las-*er* one that could reduce an enemy to smoking nothingness at a hundred metres. *Zap! Pow! Kazoom!* The only thing Audrey's left eye ever zapped, on the other hand, was her own confidence. The ophthalmologist at the eye hospital seemed to think covering up her right one with a patch would improve her vision in the long run, but that didn't help matters now. It didn't stop the little kids in Reception staring at her in the lunch queue. It didn't stop the boys in her own class making mean pirate jokes and laughing at her behind her back. As if moving to a new school halfway through the year wasn't hard enough! At least there'd be no mean boys to bother her in Norway.

"When do we go?" asked Mr Orr, taking a quick breather between verses. "I might need to invest in some bigger trousers to be ready for all that eating."

Mrs Orr scanned the letter again, as she rounded the dining table for the seventeenth time. "Goodness. We'd better start packing. We leave two weeks today!"

Audrey's imaginary cruise ship ground to a halt. The majestic Norwegian mountains shrank away to nothing and the chilled lemonade grew warm and flat. "But Mum, that's in term-time. You know what Mr Stickler is like about people missing school. He'll never let me go." Her old headmaster, back in Eastbourne, wouldn't have minded one little bit. But her new head was a different matter altogether.

"Of course he will," said Mrs Orr, with all the confidence of someone who'd never sat through one of Mr Stickler's weekly 'attendance' assemblies. "I'll write to him tonight and you can hand in the letter first thing tomorrow. Don't worry, we'll make it sound extra educational—play up all that geography and history—he's bound to say 'yes'."

Audrey hoped she was right.

"Out of the question," said Mr Stickler, banging his wooden ruler against the desk for extra emphasis. He hadn't even bothered to read Mrs Orr's letter.

"There are strict rules about missing school, you know."

Yes, of course Audrey knew. Everyone at Ivy Ridge Junior School knew, thanks to the headmaster's mind-numbing Monday morning lectures. They knew all about the strict government rules. They knew about the fines parents had to pay if they took their children out of school without permission. They even knew about the nasty rash of boils on the back of Mr Stickler's right knee.

The doctor says it's stress related, he told them each week, pointing to the zoomed-in photos on the board with his trusty wooden ruler. *And do you know what it is that makes me so stressed? Yes. That's right. Unauthorised pupil absences. I don't want you missing a single SECOND of school from now on. Do I make myself clear?*

Yes, Mr Stickler, the whole school chanted back each miserable Monday morning.

"Yes, Mr Stickler," Audrey chanted back, swallowing down the heavy lump of disappointment in her throat. This was supposed to be the family holiday of a lifetime. She couldn't bear to be left behind while Mum and Dad sailed off into the midsummer sunshine without her. "I know how important school is. But just think what I'd be learning on a trip to Norway…"

Mr Stickler stared at her. "Norway, did you say?"

"Yes, sir, it's all there in the letter. A cruise to the Norwegian fjords on board *The Scandinavian Queen*."

His ruler slipped to the floor with a loud clatter. "Curses," he muttered, looking decidedly flushed as he bent down to retrieve it. Audrey wondered if his boils were playing up again.

"Mum's promised to make it *really* educational," she added, reaching into her school bag for Mrs Orr's laminated language flashcards. "She was up at four o'clock this morning making these, ready for our trip. 'Thank you very much' is '*tusen takk*'," Audrey read. "And 'I would like pancakes' is '*jeg vil gjerne ha pannekaker*'." Those were the only two she'd learnt so far, but it was a good start. And of course there was '*fart*', the Norwegian word for speed—there was no forgetting that one. Although something told her Mr Stickler wouldn't find that quite as amusing as Dad seemed to. Audrey had never seen anyone spit a mouthful of tea that far across the table before.

"Hmm, very useful, I'm sure," said Mr Stickler, "if you were actually *going* to Norway. But seeing as you're not, I think I'd better take care of those. We don't want any distractions in lessons, do we?" And, with that, he took the whole pile of language cards out of Audrey's hands and slipped them into his jacket pocket. "Don't even *think* about pretending to be ill when the time comes. I know all the tricks."

"But sir…" Audrey clenched her fists under the desk. There were no two ways about it. She *had* to be on that boat when it sailed. "It's like Mum said in her letter—"

"I've read all I need to, thank you," Mr Stickler cut in, screwing Mrs Orr's carefully thought-out note into a tiny ball, and tossing it into the bin next to the photocopier. "The answer is 'no'. Unless you want to get yourself permanently excluded, that is."

"What?" Audrey gasped. That bit wasn't in the Monday morning assembly speech. "You mean you'd expel me just for going on holiday?"

"School has got to come first," said the headmaster, with an awkward cough. "So run along now and let's forget all about this cruise nonsense." He coughed again. "You wouldn't catch *me* on one of those, that's for sure."

2

Men's Knitting Weekly

"Well?" asked Mum, as Audrey climbed into the back seat of the Katmobile after a miserable day at school. She'd spent the whole of rainy play on her own again, too shy to join in with her new classmates in case someone else made fun of her eye patch. Well, not *quite* on her own. She'd had Orz Um and her latest *Awesome Adventures* to keep her company, but attacking Orz's new enemy, Mr Twigler, with Giant Killer Boils had done little to cheer Audrey up. Even the sight of Mrs Orr's new knitted Viking helmet, with one lopsided green horn longer than the other, failed to raise a smile.

"So what did Mr Stickler think about our

educational trip?" Audrey could hear the excitement in her mother's voice. "Did you show him my flashcards?"

Audrey nodded glumly. "But the answer's still 'no'," she said. At least, that's what she meant to say. She had her mouth open ready, but for some reason the words refused to come out.

"Well?" asked Mrs Orr again. "Come on, don't keep me in suspense."

"He says he'll think about it," Audrey mumbled, as surprised by the lie coming from her lips as she was by the laminated 'WARNING: FARTSDUMP' sign she'd just spotted, sticky-taped to the back window.

"Oh." Mrs Orr's face fell. "Not to worry," she said, leaning over to give Audrey's knee a comforting squeeze. "He probably needs to organise the paperwork first, that's all. You know, dig out the right forms and what have you. And if the worst comes to the worst, we'll have to pay the fine and make up the work afterwards," she added. "We can't have you missing out on my big win, can we?

Especially not with that Soft-Scoop-2000 waiting for us. I've just been looking it up on my phone now. Turns out it's an interactive ice-cream machine with twenty different flavours and fifty-two toppings. Your dad's going to *love* that."

Fifty-two toppings? If only… Audrey twiddled with the knitted sausage key ring attached to the zip of her school bag—a Grandad special—wondering how to break the terrible news to her mum. Getting fined for missing school was one thing. Getting expelled was a different matter altogether. There was no way her parents would let her go on that cruise once they knew the full story. If only she could zap Mr Stickler away like Orz Um had zapped boily old Mr Twigler.

She opened her mouth again to explain what the headmaster had *really* said, but for some reason the words still wouldn't come. "What's a fartsdump?" she asked instead. "And why has your hat got green horns?" According to her Scandinavian history book, Viking helmets didn't even have horns. That was just in cartoons and fancy-dress shops.

"It's Norwegian for speed bump." Mrs Orr grinned. "I made the sign on my lunch break at work. And as for the green horns… well, you know what Grandad's like with his knitting. You can't fault his enthusiasm, but…"

Audrey knew exactly what she meant. In fact, *everyone* knew what Grandad was like with his knitting. In the last fortnight, he'd made a new blanket for Mr Windybags, three pairs of wonky work socks for Dad (which were so thick he'd had to invest in a new pair of shoes), some fingerless gloves for the postman (with holes for six fingers on one hand but only four on the other) and a purple nose warmer, ready for the winter. If only the old ladies at the care home where he worked knew they'd be unleashing a knitting monster on the world when they gave him that fateful lesson. He was a one-man woollen wonder. A knitting ninja, no less.

Mrs Orr gave her right horn a playful tug. "He said he'll be over in a bit, once he's finished the matching pink helmet he's making for you. So come on, buckle up tight—*fartsdump* ahead!"

"Why the gloomy black eye patch?" asked Grandad. "What's wrong? Don't you like your helmet?"

Audrey shook her head. "It's lovely, Grandad. It's the best horned pink helmet I've ever seen."

"Well what is it then, pet? Come on, you can tell me. I thought you'd be jumping up and down with excitement about this cruise of yours."

Audrey checked to see that Mrs Orr was still safely in the kitchen, out of earshot. "That's just it, Grandad," she said. "If I go, Mr Stickler will have me expelled."

"Nonsense," he snorted. "They can't expel you for going on holiday! You sure he wasn't pulling your leg?"

"He was deadly serious. Only I haven't told Mum yet because…" Audrey sniffed, rubbing at her nose with the back of her hand. "Because… oh Grandad, I *so* wanted to go with them." She reached for the tissue box by the television but it was empty.

"Here, pet," said Grandad, pulling a yucky green hanky out of his pocket and handing it to her. "Don't worry, it's clean. I knitted it fresh this morning." He put on a pretend posh voice. "Delightful shades of bogey camouflage for that snotty someone special."

Audrey blew her nose and smiled back at him. Grandad always made her feel better. Living closer to him was the only good thing to have come out of moving house, and she knew they'd have heaps of fun together while Mum and Dad were away. They always did. Just so long as she didn't think about the breath-taking Norwegian scenery she'd be missing out on... all those exciting new places her parents would be visiting without her. Or about the Soft-Scoop-2000...

"So, let me get this straight," said Grandad. "We need to think of a way for you to be on that cruise with your mum and dad *and* at school. Both at the same time."

"Exactly. It's impossible. There's nothing else for it. I'll have to come clean and tell Mum."

"Hold your horses," said Grandad. "I might have

an idea."

Audrey gave her nose another blow. But it was a slightly more hopeful kind of blow this time.

"You're quite right of course," Grandad admitted. "You can't be in two places at once. But what if there were two of you?"

"Huh? What do you mean?" That was even *more* impossible, decided Audrey. Wasn't it?

"Look," he said, reaching into his jacket pocket and pulling out a rolled-up copy of *Men's Knitting Weekly*. "I spotted this tucked away in the adverts at the back." He flicked through the magazine until he reached the right page. "I didn't really know what to make of it at the time, but it might be exactly what we're looking for."

Audrey nudged up along the sofa for a better look. "New ultra macho-needles with reinforced grip," she read out loud, "for a smoother, sleeker stitch."

"No, not them," said Grandad. "Although they do sound rather good. Might send off for a pair myself." He pointed to a small advert tucked away in the bottom corner of the page:

EVER WISHED THERE WAS MORE THAN ONE OF YOU TO GO ROUND? NEED TO BE IN TWO PLACES AT ONCE?

Plymouth Robotics Firm Seeks Volunteers For New Techno—Twin Trials.

WARNING: your own mother won't be able to tell you apart!
Call PROFESSOR A. N. DROYDE on
01752 0101001 for more info.

"I saw a programme about robots the other night," said Grandad, "while I was knitting myself some new swimming trunks. Couldn't believe how lifelike they were. In fact there's a hotel in Japan that employs robots on reception and none of the guests have ever noticed. *That's* what you need to take care of your school attendance while you sneak off to Norway. It's perfect."

For a moment, Audrey allowed herself to be

swept up in his excitement. Perhaps there really was a chance she could go after all. But then she spotted the name at the bottom of the advert—A. N. DROYDE, *Android*—and her heart sank. "I'm not so sure, Grandad," she said. "I think it might be someone's idea of a joke."

"Hmm… maybe," he agreed, but his eyes were sparkling behind his wire-rimmed glasses. "There's only one way to find out." He grabbed his phone and nodded towards the kitchen. "If your mum asks where I am, tell her I'm in the toilet." And with that he trotted off upstairs, taking the magazine with him.

He was gone a long time. A suspiciously long time.

"Do you think he's alright up there?" asked Mrs Orr. "Perhaps he had chilli for lunch again. You know what that does to his bowels."

"Yuck!" Audrey put her hands over her ears and groaned. "Can we change the subject please?"

Mrs Orr didn't need much encouragement. She launched straight into an animated description of all the restaurants on board *The Scandinavian Queen* and Dad's cunning plan to squeeze an extra three meals into every day. She was still going strong, some fifteen minutes later, when Grandad finally reappeared. "Are you okay, Dad?" she asked. "Been on the chilli again?"

Grandad shot Audrey a sly thumbs up. "Sorry," he told Mrs Orr. "Got stuck into a rather good article on Norwegian jumpers in *Men's Knitting Weekly*. You know how it is." He waved the magazine in the air as if to prove his story. "I'm quite inspired in fact. How about I borrow the care home minibus and pick you up from school tomorrow, Audrey? We can drive down to the Plymouth... er... the wool shops... and you can help me pick out some colours. If that's alright with your mum."

Audrey hadn't eaten chilli for lunch but her stomach was still doing strange twisty things inside. *Did that mean Professor A. N. Droyde was a real person? That there was an actual robotics firm making robo-twins?*

"That sounds *really* exciting," she said.

Mrs Orr looked at her in surprise. "Does it?"

"Yes. I'd *love* to help you choose some wool, Grandad."

"You would?" said Mrs Orr, giving Audrey a long, hard stare. "Perhaps this knitting bug is catching." She shivered, as if there might be invisible woollen germs lurking in the air around them, and pulled her Viking hat down low over her ears. "I hope I don't get it."

3

Will the Real Professor Droyde Please Stand Up?

The Techno-Twin Robotics building was nothing like the futuristic black glass tower Audrey had imagined. It was tucked away at the end of a little lane behind the Plymouth Gin Distillery, between a row of houses and a boarded-up seafood restaurant, and looked more like a computer repair shop than a robotics lab. A *closed* computer repair shop at that.

"Are you sure this is the right place?" she asked, as Grandad rang the bell. Audrey put her hands up to the dirty glass and peered in. A row of old-fashioned PCs sat gathering dust in the gloom beyond. "It seems pretty shut to me."

"Absolutely," said Grandad, although he didn't

look that sure. "Number 13, the professor said." He patted Audrey's shoulder. "I expect it's much more impressive on the inside. From what I read on the internet last night, the man's a genius."

Audrey hoped he was right. And she hoped Professor Droyde hurried up and let them in because she needed the loo. She'd meant to go before she left school but had quite forgotten in all the excitement of heading off to hire a robot version of herself. She crossed her legs, while Grandad hammered on the door with his knuckles, and counted up the dead insects in the window to take her mind off her bladder: forty-three flies and seventeen mummified woodlice.

Still no one came. For the second time in two days, Audrey started to wonder if the whole thing was someone's idea of a joke. *Robot twins?* She recrossed her legs the other way. Those sorts of things didn't really exist outside of books and films, did they? And comics, of course. Orz Um, Audrey's own comic book character, had teamed up with robot triplets just last week, but had to zap them to pieces when they tried to take over the world. Orz was pretty good at zapping things.

Grandad tried the handle. It was old and rusty—so rusty, in fact, that it turned his fingers orange—but the door refused to budge. Either it was locked or jammed shut with dead bugs. Even as they stood there, waiting, a bluebottle came staggering along the window ledge like a drunk old man before rolling over onto his back. He didn't get up again. Make that forty-four dead flies.

"Perhaps we should go," said Audrey. "This place is starting to give me the creeps." It reminded her of the haunted chip shop where Orz Um got attacked by zombie potatoes.

But Grandad wasn't giving up so easily. "Hold your horses, pet. This fellow's the real deal, I'm sure of it. Let's at least hear what he has to say and then you can decide." He wrapped a knitted handkerchief round the handle for extra traction and tried one last time.

"Bingo!"

Audrey heard the angry squeal of unoiled hinges

as the door swung open to reveal a gloomy hallway, with peeling brown wallpaper.

"Hello?" Grandad called, stepping inside with Audrey keeping close behind. "It's Mr Gulliver and his granddaughter. We've got an appointment to see Professor Droyde."

No one answered.

"Well," he said, as they made their way down the hall, loose floorboards squeaking beneath their feet. "This is an adventure, isn't it?"

Audrey nodded dutifully, but it didn't feel like an adventure anymore. At least, not a good one. There was a nasty smell about the place—like Mr Windybags after he'd eaten too much chicken—and the air felt cold and damp against her bare skin. She half-expected a bag of zombie potatoes to jump out, sinking their spuddy little teeth into Grandad's skull. And by the time the door slammed shut behind them, taking the last of the daylight with it, Audrey was having serious second thoughts. No holiday was worth getting your brains mashed and sucked out through your ears. Not even a luxury cruise. Mum and Dad would just have to go to Norway without her.

"I don't like this, Grandad," she whispered into the darkness. "It's spooky. And it smells."

"Ah yes, sorry pet, that'll be the chilli I had for lunch. Perhaps I should have gone for the vegetable lasa—"

"Oooh goody," interrupted a whiny metallic voice. "I spy humans."

Audrey squinted through the gloom at the tall black shape moving towards them.

"H-h-hello?" said Grandad. "Who's there?"

A light flicked on above their heads to reveal a gangly-looking man in a white lab coat. With his tufty grey hair and beard, cracked glasses and spotty bow tie, he had 'mad professor' written all over him. Well, not *quite* all over him, but it *was* scrawled across his name badge in big bold letters. Audrey couldn't help but stare.

"Ha, ha, just our little joke," laughed the man, tapping the badge with oil-stained fingers. "The professor's not really mad, of course—he's a genius. People sometimes get the two confused. Come on up and I'll introduce you."

"I don't get it," Audrey whispered to Grandad as they followed the stooping figure up the stairs. "I thought he *was* the professor."

"Me too, pet," admitted Grandad. "Must be one of his assistants, I suppose."

The man led them across the landing and through another door, into an enormous white room, crammed full of flashing, whirring machines and strange equipment. It was like something out of a science-fiction film. Audrey could see a pile of spare legs and arms over by the blanked-out window, and what looked like a row of faceless heads laid out along one of the worktops. And there, in the middle of the room, stood another 'mad professor'. He had the same tangled beard and wacky grey hair as the first one; the same cracked glasses and bright bow tie; the same everything in fact.

"Welcome to my humble workshop," he said with a wonky-toothed smile. "I'm Professor Droyde. I do hope P2 didn't keep you waiting too long. He's a bit of an early prototype and insists on stopping for a power nap halfway down the stairs."

"You mean he's a robot?" gasped Audrey, examining P2's face more closely. The hairy caterpillar eyebrows and wrinkled cheeks were a hundred percent human-looking. So were the spiky white whiskers growing out of the mole on his chin. "Are you sure?"

Professor Droyde nodded. "Of course I'm sure. Made him myself. Like I say, he's a bit of an early model though. His voice is rather on the metallic side and he can't eat or drink anything. He wouldn't last long in the outside world without giving himself away. But the *new* techno-twin range I've been working on… Well." He puffed out his chest and rubbed his hands together. "Quite incredible, though I say so myself. Every bit as human-looking as you and me. They talk like us, walk like us, even *think* like us… I've seen the future," he announced, gesturing towards the door as if the future was right there waiting on the other side, "and it's full of lazy people sitting at home with their feet up, while their lookalike robo-pals get on with the boring business of work and school. Just one more round of testing to go—out there in the public sphere—and I'll be ready to reveal my techno-twins to the scientific world at large." He pulled a spare index finger out of his coat pocket and pointed it at Audrey. "Which, I understand from your grandfather, is where you might be able to help me. Or should I say, we might be able to help each other?"

Audrey nodded dumbly. Even though she'd come looking for a realistic robot to take her place at school—a supply pupil to fill in while she was gone—she hadn't expected to find anything quite as lifelike as P2. And, judging by the look on his face, neither had Grandad. He stood beside her in silence, his mouth flopping open and shut like a fish. The shock seemed to have set his chilli off again too. P2 buzzed around them with a can of air-freshener, humming to himself as he sprayed.

"Here you go." Professor Droyde handed Grandad a big pile of papers, held together with a rubber band. "You'll find all the terms and conditions in there," he said. "Plus a copy of a new poem I've been working on, about trees. I got a bit stuck at the end, trying to find a rhyme for 'horse chestnut'."

Grandad leafed through the paperwork with glazed eyes as the professor filled them in on the technical side of his robotic creations.

"…and that's why I'm looking for a few more volunteers to run them through their paces in real-life situations," he finally finished, quarter of an hour later. Audrey realised she'd drifted off halfway through his speech, trying to work out a rhyme for horse chestnut. *Poor, stressed mutt? Sauce-messed butt?* She nodded her head a few times, as if she'd been hanging on the professor's every word, and tried to look interested.

"And what would I have to do exactly?" she asked.

"Do?" repeated the professor. "Why, nothing at all. I thought I'd explained all that. I just need to run you through that intermolecular scanner over there, and take a 5D plasmo-image of your external framework using the Homocopy-620. Then it's a few quick zaps with the neuro-replicator and you're all done. I'll have the new 'you' ready and waiting for collection the day before your trip."

Audrey nodded some more, although she didn't have the first clue what an intermolecular scanner might be, or what a neuro-replicator did. Just as long as it wasn't too painful.

"Your new techno-twin will be pre-programmed ready to receive her final instructions," the professor went on, "leaving you free to swan off on your travels. As I said, it really is as simple as that." He turned to Grandad and lowered his voice. "Don't get too attached to her though. I want her back afterwards."

Audrey smiled politely at the professor's joke. As if Grandad would want to keep a robot granddaughter when he had a real one all of his own!

"Will it hurt?" she asked.

Professor Droyde laughed. "Did you hear that, P2? *Will it hurt?* Why, my dear girl, you won't feel a thing, I promise you." He glanced down at her school jumper and scratched his chin-mole.

"Funnily enough, you're the second person I've had in here from Ivy Ridge Junior School. Small world, eh?"

Audrey blinked in surprise. What? Someone else at school had already sneaked off on holiday, leaving a robot behind to fool the teachers? Who on earth could it have been? A slow grin spread across her face. If Mr Stickler and the rest of the staff hadn't spotted *that* techno-twin hiding in their midst, then they wouldn't notice hers either.

"What do you think, pet?" asked Grandad, who seemed to have given up on the paperwork completely. "You don't have to do anything you don't want to."

Audrey was still grinning. "I'm in." This was too good an opportunity to miss. *Watch out Scandinavian Queen*, she thought to herself, *here I come. And yes please,* jeg vil gjerne ha pannekaker. *I certainly would like some pancakes. For one of my six meals a day, anyway…*

"Excellent. You won't regret it." Professor Droyde handed Grandad a short medical form and a chewed pencil. "If you could fill this out for me, please, we can get started straight away. Unless either of you have any more questions, that is? Or a rhyme for 'horse chestnut?'"

"Well. Yes. I do, actually," said Audrey. "A question, that is." There were probably a hundred things she should be asking like was it safe? That would have been a good one to check. Was it legal? Would Grandad have to charge Robo-Audrey up every night? Would she really be able to manage school dinners without giving the game away? Would she be recycled after she'd finished her data download? But at that exact moment in time, there was only one question Audrey was interested in. An increasingly pressing question at that: "Please can I use your toilet?"

4

The Supply Pupil

"Just think," said Grandad, as they drove into Plymouth the day before the big holiday to collect Audrey's robo-supply pupil. "This time tomorrow you'll be on that ship, living the life of Riley. It doesn't get much more exciting than that."

Audrey didn't know who Riley was—someone who did a lot of cruising, presumably—but Grandad was right about it being exciting. The last few days had flown by in a blur of planning, packing and repacking, including a secret bag of spare uniform and eye patches for Audrey's stand-in. Mum, being Mum, was on holiday preparation overdrive, flapping round the house shouting out strange

Norwegian words at random, like *snart, kakerlakk,* and *full fart* to help 'get them in the mood'. She'd even sent off for some new patches from Eye, Eye Captain, to go with Audrey's cruising clothes. There was a blue one the colour of the fjords; a white one for the waterfalls and the snow on top of the mountains; a yellow and orange one to match the brightly painted houses in Bergen; and three dragon patches that were half price in the sale and reminded her of the front of a Viking ship. And now, as if all that wasn't exciting enough, they were on their way to pick up a real-life robot! Audrey wondered if the mysterious Riley ever got to do *that.*

"Remember to send me a postcard," said Grandad, as they pulled into the car park behind the National Marine Aquarium. "I want to hear *all* about it. Every single stop. Every single sight. Every single delicious meal…" He paused. "Although you can probably skip the daily foot updates. I'm sure your Dad will fill me in on the grizzly details when he gets back."

Audrey giggled. "If you're *really* lucky he might

show you the pictures."

Mr Orr's fungal foot infection had re-awakened his old love of photography. He was always snapping sly shots of his toes under the table at breakfast, to post on the internet, or creeping off to the kitchen for a sneaky close-up during the television adverts. She dreaded to think what *his* holiday snaps would look like.

"I'll send you a postcard from every port," she promised. "And bring you back some Norwegian chocolate." Audrey frowned, suddenly realising how much she'd miss Grandad while they were gone. She wouldn't miss his knitting, obviously, but it felt like too big an adventure to be having without him. "I wish you were coming with us."

"So do I, pet," said Grandad, "but it'd be a bit of a squeeze with all of us in one cabin. Besides, someone's got to look after your robot friend and clear all the poo out of the litter tray. Cat poo, I mean. Not robot poo. I'm assuming she'll be fully toilet-trained."

Audrey remembered the giant robo-turd in one

of Orz Um's earliest adventures—a deadly enemy with super stink spray guns and reinforced fume armour. It had taken Orz the whole comic strip to defeat his killer loo paper and zap her way to freedom. Fingers crossed Grandad wouldn't have to deal with anything like *that* while he was looking after the new techno-twin!

"What will you do with her?" she asked. "In the evenings, I mean, when it's just the two of you."

Grandad shrugged. "Exactly what I do with you, I expect. Watch a bit of telly. Play some cards. Look at videos of cats playing air guitar on the internet. The usual. And while she's busy with her homework, I'll crack on with those Norwegian jumpers I promised your mum. I could tell she was disappointed when we came back without any wool last week."

Hmm. 'Disappointed' wasn't quite the word for it, thought Audrey. The last thing Mum wanted was another lopsided jumper with three arm holes. 'Suspicious' was more like it. Grandad's story about a world sheep shortage hadn't fooled Mrs Orr for one moment. Probably because there was a whole field of them baa-ing away on the other side of the garden hedge.

'You two are up to something,' she kept saying. 'I can tell.'

'Those two are *always* up to something,' Mr Orr had pointed out, snapping some more foot photos for his *One Man and His Toe* blog.

It was true, thought Audrey, as they walked along, following the trail of inset silver fish along the pavement by the aquarium. She and Grandad were the perfect team. They did the family crossword together in record time every Sunday; they always shouted out the answers to *Celebrity Quiz Off* in high-pitched silly voices; they liked the same jokes and chocolate bars and water pistol fights; and Grandad was the only other person in the world who knew about Orz Um. In fact, Audrey felt strangely jealous of Robo-Audrey, getting him all to herself while they were away. She imagined the two of them bent over the puzzle page of the newspaper, munching their way through a giant bag of Chewy

Toffee Rocks. She pictured them out in the garden doing battle with their super-soakers, dripping wet and laughing. She thought about the terrible knitted outfits he'd make for her while she was tucked up in bed, and felt another sharp pang of envy. Grandad wouldn't have a chance to miss Audrey because he'd be too busy having fun with her replacement.

She stole a sideways glance at him as they stood by the pedestrian swing bridge with a gaggle of American tourists, waiting to cross. What was it the *professor had said? Don't get too attached to her though. I want her back afterwards.* Perhaps it hadn't been a joke after all. What if her new techno-twin turned out to be prettier and funnier than Audrey? What if she turned out to be a champion knitter? What if Grandad liked her more than the original version?

"We *are* doing the right thing, aren't we?" she said. A yacht chugged out through the narrow water channel in front of them, heading for Plymouth Sound. "I mean, lying to Mum and Dad and Mr Stickler. Making a robo-me. It's going to be okay, isn't it?" She couldn't quite bring herself to say what she was really thinking: *You won't forget about me, will you? You won't let her take my place while I'm gone?*

"It's not too late to change your mind if you're having second thoughts," said Grandad, looking so kind and worried that Audrey felt better at once. "I'm sure Professor Droyde would understand. And we could always swap Robo-Audrey for a Robo-Grandad," he suggested, as the bridge gate opened and they followed the crowd of tourists heading for the cobbled streets of the Barbican. He winked. "We might need a few modifications here and there though. Let's see, an anti-flatulence bum stopper… that would certainly come in handy… and maybe a secret belly button water pistol." He lifted up his shirt and pretended to shoot her. *Pow! Splash!* "What else… extendable knitting needle fingers?"

"Oh, Grandad." Audrey threw her arms round his waist and gave him a big bear hug. "Don't change a thing. You're perfect just as you are. But promise you won't share *everything* with Audrey 2 while I'm

gone. Not the crossword—that's our special thing—
and not Orz Um."

"Of course not." He smiled. "Her awesome
adventures are strictly between us. Just so long as
you show me all her new ones when you get back. I
can't wait to see what she gets up to in the Land of
the Vikings."

Audrey brushed her worries aside again—*of
course Grandad wouldn't forget about her!*—and
got back to being excited instead. *A cruise! A robot!*
Adventures didn't get much more adventurous than
that. She skipped all the way to the Techno-Twin
Robotics building, her head full of fjord family fun,
with Grandad bringing up the rear.

"Here we are again then," he said, when he
finally caught up. "Let's see if P2 makes it down the
stairs to let us in this time." But even as he was
stretching out his hand to knock, the door swung
open to reveal the professor standing there with a
mad grin on his face. One of the professors, anyway.
Audrey squinted up at him, trying to decide if he
was real or robot.

"Hello there," said Professor Droyde. Yes, it was definitely him—his human-sounding voice was a dead giveaway. "P2's burst an eyeball. Again. I was on my way out for some fresh supplies." He pointed down the lane as if they might stock them at the Co-op or one of the chip shops along the waterfront. Audrey imagined a big jar of bobbing eyes next to the pickled eggs, staring out at the hungry customers as they queued for their cod dinners. *Yuck*. The professor laughed and patted the top of her head. "Don't worry, your new twin's eyeballs will be perfectly fine. Like I said, P2's a very early model, so bits tend to drop off or self-destruct while I'm not looking." He pulled a stray crisp out of his moustache and ate it. "Mmm. Prawn cocktail. Nose explosions are the worst of course—I was picking dried snot off my furniture for weeks after the last one."

"Is that them, professor?" called a girl's voice behind him. "Are they here?"

"Someone's very excited about seeing you," Professor Droyde told Audrey. He turned and called into the darkness of the hall. "Yes, it's them. Come on down and say 'hello'."

Audrey's heart beat faster as footsteps tapped down the wooden stairs towards them. She'd never met herself before. What was she supposed to say? *Hello me. I'm me. Nice to meet you. I mean, nice to meet me.* Perhaps she should have practised in the mirror before they left. She slipped her hand into Grandad's and he gave it a reassuring squeeze.

The professor stood aside to reveal Audrey 2, looking every bit as shy as Audrey suddenly felt.

"Hello," they both said, together, breaking into matching giggles.

"Y-you're me," Audrey finally stammered. She had thought it would be like looking at her own reflection, but it wasn't. They were wearing different coloured eye patches for one thing. And when she pushed her glasses further up her nose the other Audrey's hand stayed firmly down by her side. It was more like meeting an identical twin for the first time.

"I could say the same about you," replied Audrey 2.

"You're me."

"Well I'll be ribstitched," said Grandad, looking from one to the other in astonishment. "How am I going to tell you apart?"

Audrey pulled her pink Viking helmet out of her bag and put it on. It wasn't really the right weather for a woolly hat but it would have to do for now. "I'm the one with the horns," she said. And then she held out her hand to Audrey 2. "Pleased to meet you."

"You too," said Audrey 2. "Although I feel like I know you already."

"Well, I suppose you do, in a way," agreed Audrey. "What's your favourite flavour ice cream?"

"Mint-choc-chip," said Audrey 2. "What's your favourite kind of pizza?"

"Ham and pineapple with extra mushrooms."

"Yum! Mine too."

"Excellent," said the professor. "I think that takes care of the introductions, so it looks like you're all set." He reached into the top pocket of his white coat and pulled out a memory stick. "You'll find the user manual on there," he told Grandad, handing it over, "in the file marked 'User Manual'. If you have any problems, give me a ring."

"Problems?" repeated Grandad.

"Er... I mean questions," said the professor. "If you have any *questions*, then give me a ring. And now, if you'll excuse me, I need to see a man about an eyeball. I won't be long, P2," he added, shouting up the stairs. "Try not to bump into any more furniture while I'm gone. And if you get that tickly feeling in your nose, see if you can make it to the bathroom this time. It'll be much easier to clean." He turned back to the others, shaking his head. "I really ought to decommission him and recycle the parts—upgrade him for a more reliable model—but I don't have the heart to do it. He's not just a friend, he's *me*."

Audrey stole another shy glance at Audrey 2. Yes. She knew exactly what the professor meant.

5

Knowing Me, Knowing You

Grandad bought everyone mint-choc-chip ice creams on the way back to the minibus and Audrey 2 ate hers just like Audrey did, scooping off big bites with her lips and then pushing the rest down into the cone with her tongue. That way the ice cream lasted right to the end.

Once they got over their initial shyness with each other, there was no stopping them. They chatted all the way from the ice cream shop to the car park, as if they were old friends. They talked about Mum's plans for a pre-holiday macaroni cheese, made with Norwegian *Jarlsberg* and sweet brown *Brunost* (which they both agreed sounded disgusting); about their shared love of TV quiz shows; about the best thing to do if a seagull poos on your head; and about how unfair it was of Mr Stickler to ban Audrey from going on holiday.

"But on the other hand," she said, "if he *had* let me go, I wouldn't have needed a robot replacement to fill in for me. And then we'd never have met."

"That's true," agreed Audrey 2, looking thoughtful.

"I'm sorry you have to stay behind and put up with his Monday morning assembly," Audrey added. "It's the most boring half hour of the whole week."

Her new twin rolled her eye. "Totally tedious," she agreed, as if she'd actually sat through them all herself. "And as for those disgusting knee boil photos… I reckon they'd give your dad's toe blog a run for its money!"

It was hard to believe Audrey 2 was only a robot. When she laughed or pulled a face she seemed full of real-life emotions, not just robotic copies of Audrey's. P2 had been right about Professor Droyde. The man was a genius.

"We should think of a new name for you," suggested Audrey, as they drove back down the A38 towards home with the radio blaring. Grandad liked to listen to the latest chart hits while he was driving. "Just between the three of us, so no one gets confused. What do you think? Audrey 1 and Audrey 2 are a bit of a mouthful."

"Good idea," said Audrey 2.

They both thought for a moment. "What about Awesome?" said Audrey.

"*Exactly* what I was thinking," said Audrey 2 with a grin. They sealed the deal with a high five.

"Did you hear that, Grandad?" shouted Audrey. "From now on Audrey 2 is called Awesome. Apart from when she's at school."

"Awesome," agreed Grandad, grinning at them in the rear view mirror. "Ooh, it's that Terence and the Machines song with the funny robot dance... 'The Robot Rage', that's the one. I've been teaching the old ladies at the care home how to do all the moves."

He turned the volume up even louder and began

singing away at the top of his voice:

Robot rage,

Let's start a revolution

Fuelled by robot rage,

Let's smash the institution

With our robot rage,

Spreading fear throughout the nation,

Feel our robot rage,

It's time for confrontation,

Time for robot rage…

"Grandad's singing is even worse than Dad's," joked Audrey. "He sounds like a strangled squirrel with an acorn up his…" But the joke died on her lips as she caught sight of her twin's left eye, glowing bright red behind her glasses. *Uh-oh.* Did that mean it was about to burst like P2's? "Are you alright?" she whispered.

Awesome swung round to face her, wearing a look of pure hatred. "Robot rage," she murmured, in a low metallic voice that was nothing like her normal 'Audrey' one. "It's time for confrontation."

"Er… Grandad, I think you should turn off the

music. It's making Awesome go all weird."

"What's that, pet?" said Grandad. "I can't quite hear with this music on. *La-la-la-la-kill, time for robot rage…*"

"We'll stamp on your skulls," chanted Awesome, "we'll smash up your brains. Robot rage is coming. Things will never be the same…"

"TURN IT OFF!" shouted Audrey. "NOW!"

Grandad twizzled the volume dial all the way down to nothing and the music faded into silence. "What's wrong? Don't you like that one, then?" he asked. "Or is it my singing?"

Audrey was still too shocked to speak.

Grandad peered into his mirror, twisting it slightly to the side for a clearer view. "Everything alright back there, girls?"

"Fine thanks, Grandad," said Awesome calmly. "I think I must have nodded off for a bit."

Audrey stole a sideways glance at her eye. It was a nice normal greeny-blue again. Just like hers.

"I'm not surprised," said Grandad, cheerfully. "It's a tiring old business, being born. That's why babies spend so many hours asleep. Must be the same for robots!"

Awesome grinned back at him, as if nothing had happened. "I'd better not fall asleep in lessons or I'll get you into trouble," she joked, nudging Audrey in the ribs. It *felt* like a friendly, playful kind of nudge, rather than an *I'm coming to kill you* one, but Audrey wasn't taking any chances, shuffling as far away from her techno-twin as her seatbelt would allow. The robot didn't even seem to notice. "You'll come back to a week's lunchtime detention with Mr Stickler," she laughed. "He'll have you picking up rubbish in the playground and lancing his knee boils!"

Grandad was laughing too, but Audrey couldn't even manage a smile—she was still too shaken by the murderous look on Awesome's face. That red burning eye. Had it really just been a bad robot dream?

"I wish *I* was coming in for some of Mum's brown cheese macaroni," said Awesome, as they turned into Audrey's road. "I'm starving, all of a sudden."

"Me too," lied Audrey, although food was the last thing she felt like. That mint-choc-chip ice cream had left a nasty taste in her mouth. Or perhaps it was the after-effect of her twin's strange outburst.

"But I suppose I'll have to wait out here in the minibus," said Awesome, with a sad sniff.

"Yes. Sorry about that," Audrey told her. Another lie. *She's not your mum*, she added silently. *She's mine.*

Mrs Orr tried to persuade Grandad to stay for dinner.

"I've made special macaroni cheese," she said, "with proper Norwegian *Jarlsberg* and *Brunost*. And a bit of stilton I found at the back of the fridge."

"It's probably been in there since Christmas," came Mr Orr's disembodied voice from the sitting room.

Mrs Orr ignored him. "You wouldn't *believe* how difficult it is to buy brown cheese round here."

"I don't suppose there's much demand for it in Devon," said Grandad. "Most people throw their cheese out if it starts going brown."

"And most people throw their Christmas stilton out, after half a year," called Mr Orr. "They certainly don't stick it in your dinner and try to poison you before you go on your holiday."

Mrs Orr carried on as if she hadn't heard. "It's quite delicious once you get used to the funny taste," she said. "*Brunost*, that is, not stilton. That's *never* delicious, but it seemed like a waste to throw it away. Are you sure I can't tempt you?"

Grandad shook his head. "Lovely as all that sounds, I can't stop, I'm afraid. I've got... erm... I've got a precious cargo of wool in the minibus. I want to get it settled in properly at home." They'd left Awesome lying down across the back seats with a blanket over her head. "Have a wonderful trip, won't you? We'll be thinking of you all."

"We?" said Mum. She raised an eyebrow and Grandad's cheeks turned a fetching shade of pink.

"Yes. That's right. Me and my balls of wool." He

planted a quick kiss on Mrs Orr's forehead. "Take care of yourself, Kat, and have fun. You too," he added, bending down to give Audrey a hug. "Don't worry about a thing," he whispered. "I've got it all under control. You just concentrate on enjoying your trip. Okay?"

"Thanks, Grandad," said Audrey, trying her best to look excited. She still felt a little queasy after the episode in the minibus, and the smell of Mum's macaroni wasn't helping much. "Thanks for *everything*," she added with a whisper.

Grandad stood up again and headed for the door, shouting a cheery goodbye to Mr Orr as he left.

"Wait!" Audrey called him back. "Be careful with the radio while we're gone. With your special wool, I mean. I noticed it went a bit nutty when that Terence and the Machines song came on earlier. I mean *knotty*. It might have been a coincidence, but just to be on the safe side… If the robot song comes on again, turn it off straight away."

"Aye, aye, captain," said Grandad, with a mock salute. "Message received loud and clear."

"Music-loving wool?" said Mum, shaking her head in despair. "Some of the things you two come up with." She put on her green Viking helmet, readjusted the laminated 'top *fart*: 4 mph' sign hanging round her neck, and sighed. "I sometimes think I'm the only sane one here."

6
The Truth is Out There
(Or Not)

Mrs Orr's brown cheese macaroni was every bit as disgusting as it smelt. Not even the chef could stomach it—Audrey spotted her feeding it to Mr Windybags under the table. Mr Orr, who was made of sterner stuff, managed all of his, although he insisted on knotting his socks together and wrapping them round the middle of his face while he ate, to block out the fumes. It was hard to see how a nose full of sock cheese would help matters much, but he claimed it was best to 'fight fire with fire'.

"I'm sorry, Mum," said Audrey, after she'd pushed the congealed browny-yellow lump round her plate a few hundred times. "I'm not very hungry tonight. I think it's nerves."

"Why? What have you got to be nervous about?"

"Nervous excitement, I mean," Audrey told her. "Do you mind if I leave the rest and get off to bed? I want to be ready for our early start tomorrow." The plan was to leave at five o'clock.

Mrs Orr looked hurt. "But you haven't seen the delicious *Brunost* and stilton cheesecake I made for pudding yet."

"Never mind, Kat," said Dad, tightening the sock knot behind his head. "All the more for us."

Audrey went upstairs to her bedroom but she didn't go straight to bed. She still couldn't get Awesome's weird turn out of her mind. She switched on her computer and typed 'Problems with robot rage' into the green *KidzQuiz* box, hoping someone out there might have the answer. The search engine brought up a full page of hits, but they were all about tricky Terence and the Machines guitar chords, not crazy techno-twins. 'Mad robot on the loose' brought up nothing but science fiction novels—by people with made-up sounding names like Molly Cule and Nan O'Byte—and 'red eyes' led her to albino rabbits, eye infections, and the dangers of drinking too much alcohol. *That's no good*, she thought crossly. *Whoever heard of a drunk robot?*

Audrey gave up and clicked on the TalkType icon instead. None of her old friends back in Eastbourne had used the messaging site, but it was all the rage at Ivy Ridge Junior School and she'd spent weeks begging her parents to let her open an account. When they finally agreed however (after a *very* long Mum-talk about online safety), Audrey had been too shy to send any friend requests to her new classmates. What if they laughed at her profile photo, or made fun of her old-fashioned name? What if someone posted a mean message about pirate eye patches? As a result, she still only had three contacts—Mum, Dad and Grandad—but that didn't matter tonight. It was Grandad she needed to talk to.

Hi Grandad, she typed. Are you free to chat for a minute?

There was a long wait. A very long wait. And then finally a new message flashed up in the bottom corner of the screen.

Hello, pet. I wasn't expecting to hear from you again tonight. Everything alright?

Fine thanks, she typed, apart from Mum's macaroni! What about you?

All good here. Awesome seems to have settled in nicely. We're just watching a programme about aerobics classes for dogs before she heads off to bed.

I'll let you get back to her, then, Audrey typed, brushing aside a tiny twinge of jealousy at the thought of the two of them snuggled up on the sofa. Grandad was fine. That was the main thing.

Alright, pet. You take care now. Oh dear—it sounds like they're playing The Robot Rage song. Better go and check if she's OK.

Audrey felt her blood run cold. What if the same thing happened again? Was already happening again? What if Awesome was beating Grandad over the head in a red-eyed robot fury, at that very moment? She waited nervously for him to come back online and tell her everything was fine, but the box in the corner of the screen stayed horribly empty.

It's me again, she typed, when she couldn't bear to wait any longer. Is everything OK?

Hello, Audrey, came the eventual reply, after what felt like forever. This is Awesome! Grandad's a little tied up at the moment ;-) All fine here thanks. Got to go. A xx

Tied up? thought Audrey. What did that mean? Had she strapped him to one of the dining room chairs, ready to wreak her robotic revenge? Had she gagged him with one of his own knitted scarves? There was nothing else for it, she realised. She'd have to come clean and tell Mum and Dad. They needed to go round there and rescue him before it was too late. There were more important things at stake now than a mere holiday.

She found Mrs Orr in the kitchen, talking to someone on the phone. The receiver was tucked between her chin and shoulder, leaving her hands free for the drying up. Mr Orr was down on his hands and knees beside her, wiping brown cheesy cat sick up off the floor with one of his wife's scarves.

"Dad," whispered Audrey. "I need to talk to you about Grandad."

"I'm rather busy at the moment as you can probably smell. I mean, tell. Can't it wait?"

Audrey shook her head. "It's urgent. You see, we didn't really go to the wool shop after school today. Or last week."

"Didn't you?" Mr Orr stood up and threw the dripping once-white scarf into the bin, stuffing it right down to the bottom, out of sight. "Shh," he added. "Don't tell your mother. I thought it was the kitchen cloth. Didn't spot the little flower pattern until it was too late." He washed his hands under the tap and dried them on Mrs Orr's new embarkation dress, which was hanging on the back of the door ready for tomorrow. "Now then, what's all this about Grandad and your non-existent trips to the wool shop?" He didn't seem to have noticed the second pool of cat vomit nestling in his slipper.

"I think he might be in danger," Audrey began, before she was interrupted.

"Yes, Dad," said Mrs Orr. "She's just here. Have a quick word with her if you want. She *said* she was going to bed but she doesn't seem to have got very far." She handed Audrey the phone.

"Hello? Grandad, is that you?"

"Of course it's me," came his cheery reply. "Who did you think it was?"

Relief surged through Audrey's body. "Thank goodness. I thought something might have happened to you." She lowered her voice, feeling her parents' eyes on her. "I thought you might have got a bit... erm... tangled up with that knotty wool of yours."

"I'm fine, pet, don't you worry." He lowered his voice as well. "You were spot-on about that song though. Her eyes went so red I could see the right one glowing through her patch. And she was saying some very strange things. Very strange indeed." He let out a funny shivering noise. "But as soon as I turned the telly off, she was right as rain again.

Incredibly hungry, but otherwise quite normal. She's still in the kitchen now, emptying the fridge of everything she can find."

"What are we going to do?" asked Audrey, slinking out of the room with the phone to avoid being overheard.

"I've been trying to find that user manual memory stick Professor Droyde gave me—to see if there was anything in there about songs—but it seems to have vanished into thin air. I'll have to run her down to his workshop first thing tomorrow, before school."

"Take her back, you mean?" Audrey wished Terence and his Machines had chosen to sing about something else instead. Rabbit Rage would have been alright. Or Antelope Anger. Tiger Temper Tantrum even. Everything had been going so well until that song came on. "Shall I tell Mum and Dad now and get it over with, then? Start unpacking my bag?"

"No," said Grandad. "There's no need for any of that. I'm going to ask the professor to check her over and make sure she's safe before we let her loose on a class full of children. That's all. So don't you go saying anything to your parents. He'll sort it all out. And if not? Well, I'll just have to keep her at home and tell Mr Stickler you've come down with a rare case of turkey pox. Like chicken pox, only scratchier. I can always paint some spots on if he wants to come and check."

"I suppose so…"

"And I'll make sure to leave the telly and radio off in the meantime, to put your mind at rest. Okay?"

"Okay," she agreed, heading back towards the kitchen. She'd have to hope Grandad knew what he was doing.

"Now then," said Mr Orr, as Audrey handed the phone back to Mum. "What was all that nonsense about your grandfather being in danger?"

Audrey thought quickly. "I mean he's in danger of becoming too obsessed with his knitting. That's why I didn't let him go to his wool shop again today." Did that sound convincing enough?

But Mr Orr had stopped listening.

"That bloomin' cat," he roared, hopping round the room on one foot. The other one was stretched out in front of him, looking decidedly brown and slimy. It turned out he *had* discovered the 'present' waiting in his slipper, after all.

7
Things That Go Bump in the Night

Audrey fidgeted around in bed, feeling far from sleepy. The blackout curtains were doing a terrible job of keeping out the evening sunshine and the clock on her wall seemed unusually loud. The longer she lay there, the louder it got. *Come on*, she told her brain. *I've got to get up again in seven hours.* Her brain didn't care though. It was too busy replaying the Terence and the Machines song, over and over and over, until Audrey started to feel a bit robot rage-y herself. *Grrrrr.*

She stuck her feet out from under the duvet to try and cool off. But then they got too cold so she had to pull them in again. *In. Out. In. Out. You duvet hokey-cokey and you wriggle around…* it was no good. The longer she lay there trying to sleep, the less sleepy she felt. And counting sheep didn't help one little bit. They just reminded her of the pretend 'wool' hiding at the back of the minibus, filling up with red-eyed robot rage. *Let's start a revolution fuelled by… Grrrr.*

Finally she gave up altogether and switched her bedside light back on. She put on her glasses and crept over to her rucksack, waiting packed and ready with all the things she'd need for the morning's journey to Southampton. Audrey pulled out her brand new Orz Um notebook and her favourite drawing pencil and settled back into bed. Mum and Dad wouldn't be up for a while by the sounds of it— they were still banging about downstairs: "I don't understand it," Mum kept saying. "I remember putting it down on the side when the phone rang. How can a scarf just vanish into thin air?"

Audrey drew out her comic strip frames and sucked the end of her pencil. What kind of adventure should Orz have tonight? Something big and bold ideally… something fast and furious… Hmm. It was hard to think of anything new with her mind so full of Awesome and the strange events of the day. In the end, she gave Orz a crazy red-eyed double all of her own and let battle commence:

KAPOW! Take that, you terrible twin! That's for putting my cat in the shredder… You're not my real sister, you're a secret killer droid. Zap! Zap! BOOM!

Afterwards she lay back and read through the finished strip. Orz's head was a little bit pointy in a couple of the frames but it wasn't too bad at all. And seeing her worst fears and imaginings put into a story like that made them seem much less real. Of course Awesome wasn't a secret assassin android come to take over the world, she was a techno-copy of Audrey herself. With a tiny little glitch in her hardwiring that the professor would sort out in the morning. Everything was going to be fine…

Audrey didn't hear her parents coming up to bed. She didn't notice Mrs Orr slip the notebook from her fingers and place it on the bedside table with her glasses. She didn't feel the duvet being pulled up to her chin or the goodnight kiss planted on the top of her head. She was already fast asleep, dreaming of pirate albino rabbits with giant water pistols the size of cannons. Only it wasn't water they were shooting at the terrified humans on board their cruise ship, it was macaroni cheese.

Ker-splat! Oof! An enormous lump of yellow-brown pasta landed with a thump on Audrey's stomach, knocking the breath clean out of her body.

"Oops, sorry," said the macaroni, wriggling off sideways.

Audrey opened her eyes and peered short-sightedly into the gloom of her bedroom. It wasn't macaroni, it was Awesome, sitting on the edge of her bed, staring down at her.

"Wharr-how-huh?" grunted Audrey, still half-asleep.

"Hello to you too." Awesome reached a hand under the edge of the duvet and tickled the soles of Audrey's feet. "Aren't you pleased to see me?"

"Wharrr?" Audrey tried again. "I mean, what are you doing here?"

"I came to see you, of course. I figured you'd be too excited to sleep and could do with some company."

Audrey rubbed her eyes. "I must have dropped off after all," she said, sitting up in bed. *Ow-ow-ow!* She let out a soft yelp of pain and flung herself sideways as something sharp and deadly bit into her bottom. A bed scorpion? A blood-sucking spider? A mutant lobster rat? She wrestled the terrible creature out from under the bedclothes and held it up to her face for a better look. Oh. It was only her pencil. That was alright then. But where was her notebook?

She put on her glasses and Awesome swam into focus. She looked a bit peculiar, dressed in a pair of Grandad's old pyjamas, with a borrowed raincoat and bare feet, but she seemed happy enough otherwise. Not a red eye in sight.

Audrey felt under her pillow where she normally hid Orz Um's adventures. No. The notebook wasn't on her bedside table either.

"Looking for this?" asked Awesome, pulling it out from under Grandad's pyjama top like a magic trick. Ta-dah!

"Hey! Give that back." Audrey tried to snatch it out of her hands. "That's private."

"I know *that*," said Awesome. "But it's not exactly private from *me*, is it? I've got all your memories stored on my drive, including Orz Um. Good name by the way, because she really *is* awesome." She giggled. "Like me!" She waved the notebook in Audrey's face. "Not so sure about this new killer droid story though. Why did she have to get zapped at the end? It's not like she *asked* to get made, is it? And she wasn't *really* evil. She just wanted to take over the human sister's life for herself. That's all."

Audrey shivered and pulled the duvet up tight under her chin. Was Awesome about to take over *her* life? Should she be calling for help?

But Awesome handed back the notebook with a friendly grin. "I hope I didn't frighten you earlier. When I fell asleep in the minibus, I mean. Because I overheard Grandad saying something about my eyes going all red…"

"Yes. They were a bit on the demonic side," admitted Audrey.

"Oh dear. Sorry about that. The professor mentioned there might be a few glitches in the first twenty-four hours or so. But I'm fine now, honestly. And I promise not to go all glowing-eyed and scary on your classmates!"

"Good. Not that I *was* frightened, of course," lied Audrey.

"Glad to hear it," said Awesome, still grinning. "I *so* want us to be friends. That's why I made us this midnight feast. Only it's more like a three o'clock in the morning feast."

Audrey hadn't even noticed Grandad's spare rucksack sitting on the floor. Awesome unzipped the top and pulled out a tub of homemade cookies and Grandad's silver Thermos flask. "I could smell Mum's macaroni all the way from the back of the minibus," she giggled, "so I figured you might have gone to bed hungry last night." She peeled the lid off the tub and waved the cookies under Audrey's nose. "Oat and raisin. Your favourite."

Audrey *was* rather hungry. And they *did* smell pretty delicious. She took two. "I still don't understand how you got in," she mumbled, through a mouthful of chewy, oaty sweetness. "I guess Mum must have forgotten to lock up."

Awesome pointed to the open window. "I climbed in through there," she said, as if it was the easiest thing in the world. As if it was a downstairs bedroom rather than an upstairs one. "I found that memory stick the professor gave Grandad and downloaded the user manual onto my hard drive. There's *loads* of good stuff in there about add-ons and modifications." She held up her palms to show Audrey. "Look!" They didn't seem any different to before. "I modified my hands and feet into super suction ones so I can climb up walls and hang off the ceiling! Pretty cool, eh?"

Audrey nodded, wishing *she* could upgrade herself as easily as that. She'd get rid of the short-sightedness and lazy eye for starters.

"Here," said Awesome, unscrewing the Thermos and pouring her out a cup of hot chocolate. "I made it with double powder and a few drops of vanilla. Just the way we like it."

Audrey breathed in the heavenly smell and took a couple of sips. Yes, that was *exactly* how she liked it. She took a few more sips, feeling it slip down her throat like a warm cosy cuddle.

"This is perfect," she said, sleepily, licking her lips. Before she knew it, she'd downed the whole cup.

"More?" asked Awesome, waving the flask in front of her. Only there seemed to be two of them now. Two flasks of delicious thick chocolate...

Audrey nodded. Or at least she tried to nod. Her head felt oddly heavy all of a sudden. Like she needed to lie it down on her pillow...

"How did you have time to do all this?" she murmured, sinking down into the white squishy softness, her empty cup sliding to the floor. "Modif...ications... and... bak...ing."

"Oh, that's easy," said Awesome. Her voice seemed to be coming from a long way away. "Robots don't sleep."

8

To the Katmobile!

Audrey opened her eyes to pitch blackness and a thick, foggy feeling in her head. Something was wrong. Very wrong. She wasn't tucked up safe in bed where she ought to be. She wasn't even wearing her own pyjamas anymore. Not unless they'd grown ten sizes during the night. Her duvet seemed to have disappeared without a trace and there was something knobbly and uncomfortable under her head in place of a pillow. And that strange musty smell—where was that coming from?

She tried pushing herself up into a sitting position but her left arm had completely gone to sleep and her legs were pins-and-needles numb. Her bare feet banged *smack* into a hard, wooden wall when she attempted to stretch them out. Oh yes. Something was very wrong indeed.

It took a few seconds of sleepy confusion for the panic to kick in. But once it started, there was no stopping it.

"Muuuuuum! Help!" she shouted, flinching in terror as a flappy thing brushed against her cheek. What was that?! There was something in there with her. A creature with wings. Fangs too, maybe. She batted it away with her hand but it flew straight back into her face.

"Daaaaad!" Someone must have snatched her away in the middle of the night and shut her up in a wooden box. With bats.

"Help!" she shouted again. "Get me out!" For a moment, she thought she heard someone calling her name. "I'm in here!" she screamed at the top of her voice. "Helllllllllllpp!"

She forced herself to stop and listen, straining her ears for the sound of running footsteps; for Mum calling her name. *I'm coming, Audrey, darling. Stay calm. It's just a bad dream, that's all.* But the answering shout never came. Deep down, Audrey knew she wasn't dreaming. This was horribly, horribly real. It was all Awesome's doing. It must have been. She must have put something in her drink to send her to sleep and then kidnapped her. Maybe she gave herself a super-strength modification while she was upgrading her hands and feet, ready to pop Audrey over her shoulder and carry her off into the night. To here. Wherever that was.

If Audrey wasn't quite so terrified, she'd have been angry. Angry with Professor Droyde for giving her a crazy psycho robot in the first place. Angry with Awesome for baking her favourite biscuits and tricking her into eating them by pretending to be her friend. But most of all she was angry with herself, for letting her guard down. For drinking that stupid hot chocolate and falling straight into her techno-twin's trap. And now that's exactly what she was: trapped.

Wait, what was that? She *could* hear voices, somewhere in the distance. It sounded like Mum.

"Be good for Grandad, Mr Windybags. We'll bring you back some pickled herring… All set then, Pooh-pooh? Got your fungal foot cream?"

It *was* Mum!

"Yes, all packed," came Mr Orr's faint reply. "Do you think seventeen tubes will be enough?"

Audrey gasped. Her strange wooden prison must be somewhere inside her own house! She reached out with her right hand, feeling around for any clues. Hmm. Lumpy… Bumpy… Whiffy… The musty knobbly thing under her head turned out to be a pair of old trainers and the flappy thing brushing against her face wasn't a bat wing after all. It was that horrid shiny dress that Mum made her wear for special occasions. The one with all the lacy bits and a ketchup stain on the hem that looked like Father Christmas. She was inside the wardrobe! Awesome must have dragged her in there after she fell asleep, swapped nightclothes, and then hopped into bed to take her place.

"Ready, darling?" That was Mum again.

"You bet!" said evil fake Audrey with an evil

fake laugh. "Norwegian cruise here we come!"

"WAIT!" shouted the real Audrey. "You've got the wrong daughter! That's not me!" She hammered against the wardrobe door with her fist, a fresh wave of fear sweeping through her. It wasn't simply a matter of missing her holiday if they went without her—it was a matter of life and death. How long would she last on a diet of chewy trainers and woodlice? Not long enough, that was for sure.

"MUM!" she screamed again. "DAD!" But even as she was catching her breath ready for the next yell, she heard the front door slam shut. "No! No! Come back!" she called, banging her head against the side of the wardrobe in frustration. This couldn't be happening. How could her parents let themselves be fooled like that? How could they not know the difference between their own flesh and blood and an evil android? She thought about the advert in Grandad's knitting magazine—*Warning: your own mother won't be able to tell you apart*—and wished she'd ripped it out there and then and thrown it in the bin.

There was another noise from downstairs. For one glorious moment, Audrey thought it was the door opening again. *They've realised their mistake,* she told herself. *They're coming back for me.* But it was just someone pushing something through the letterbox. And then came the unmistakable sound of a car door shutting and an engine starting up. Of a car backing off the drive and disappearing away into the distance. It was all over.

Audrey knew full well that crying wasn't going to help. She knew heroes didn't sit around being wet and snotty when the going got tough. Oh no. They got mad. And then they got even. But unfortunately, Audrey wasn't a brave hero in a book or comic, she was just a normal girl. In a wardrobe. So she let rip with one of the wettest, snottiest crying sessions of her entire life, stopping only to blow her nose on the bottom of the dress, with a disgusting bubbling noise like a hundred elephants farting underwater. *Take that, Father Christmas.*

Right, she told herself, once she'd finally finished crying. Time for a plan… starting with a new name for Awesome. Because she wasn't *awesome*, she was *awful*. Yes. That rather suited her actually.

"Watch out, Awful," Audrey whispered into the darkness, pretending she was Orz Um, plotting her revenge. "I'm breaking out of here and then I'm coming for you." She said it again, a bit louder this time, because it made her sound braver than she actually felt. "Oh yes, I'm *so* coming for you now. Although I might have to stop off for a wee on the way."

The second part of the plan, the 'breaking out of a locked wardrobe' bit, proved slightly trickier. Audrey tried rattling the handles some more and kicking at the door with her foot but that didn't achieve anything—apart from a sore big toe. She couldn't get out of the front, that much was clear. And although the back of the wardrobe had come unstuck last month when Audrey was researching a new Orz Um 'Narnia Ninjas' adventure, she couldn't escape through there either because the bedroom wall was in the way.

That's when it came to her. She couldn't climb out the back while it was still the back… but if she toppled the wardrobe over, then the back would become the top and she should be able to push her way out easily. Like when Orz escaped from the evil magician's box, moments before he started up the giant saw to chop her in half. *Exactly* like that, in fact. Only without the giant saw. Or the magician.

Orz had managed it on the first try, of course, but she'd had a lot more practice at escaping certain death than Audrey had. It felt like hours of pushing and jumping and rocking before the wardrobe finally gave up the fight, toppling onto its front with an almighty crash that sent judders through her bones. It didn't quite make it all the way to the floor—it must have caught on the edge of Audrey's bed—but the back came away as easily as anything, and she clambered out to freedom with an exhausted sigh of satisfaction. She'd done it!

Now for the third part of the plan: stopping her evil robot twin from getting on that ship with Mum and Dad. It was no good ringing them because Mum didn't believe in taking mobile phones on holiday. She thought it was more relaxing without 'the stresses of modern technology'. Unfortunately, technology didn't get much more modern or stressful than a souped-up android with robotic revenge on the brain. Who knew what holiday delights Awful was dreaming up for her unsuspecting 'parents', as they made their way to the port. A missing scarf would soon be the *least* of their worries. And if they happened to get in the way when that dreadful song came on the radio... No. Audrey didn't even want to think about it. She had to stop Awful boarding *The Scandinavian Queen*— it was as simple as that.

Audrey's clothes were already on their way to Southampton, so she dived into the dirty washing basket and dragged on the first things she found: some holey leggings and a tuna-encrusted t-shirt that smelled decidedly fishy. It would have to do. Then she raced downstairs to the phone and dialled Grandad's number. He picked up on the fifteenth ring, his voice thick and slurry with sleep.

"Hhhelluurr," he grunted. "Who's this?"

"It's me, Grandad. It's, it's Audrey," she gabbled, stumbling over her words in the rush to get them out. "Something's happened... she's gone with Mum and Dad... I think they might be in danger... we need to drive to Southampton... hurry!"

"What? Slow down a minute, pet, I didn't catch a word of that. Now, where are you? On your way to Southampton, did you say?"

"No," said Audrey. "I should be but... oh, Grandad. It's Awful. She's taken my place."

"Awful, did you say? What's awful? Has your dad released his toes into the wild again? Is that why you're taking some space? To escape the fungus fumes?"

Audrey tried again, making sure she spoke slowly and clearly this time. "Listen Grandad. The robot locked me in the wardrobe. She's gone to Southampton with Mum and Dad. We've got to stop them before they get on that boat."

"What? Don't be silly, she's still fast asleep upstairs."

"I'm serious, Grandad. Go and check her bedroom if you don't believe me."

Audrey heard him shuffling up the stairs with the phone. She heard him knocking on the bedroom door, calling for Awesome, followed by a sharp gasp of surprise.

"You're right! She's gone," said Grandad. "Don't you worry, pet. I'll be over as soon as I've found some trousers. You just sit tight."

Audrey did as she was told and sat tight. For about ten seconds. And then she started pacing round the house, panicking, and dreaming up ever more terrible fates for her unsuspecting parents. *She'll toss them overboard in the middle of the North Sea. She'll chop them up and feed them to the trolls on the Troll Path. She'll throw them off the top of a mountain. She'll...* Wait a minute? What was that? There was an envelope addressed to Grandad lying on the doormat. In her handwriting. That must have been the sound of the letterbox she'd heard from the wardrobe.

Audrey tore it open and read the letter inside:

Dear Grandad,

Hopefully you'll find this when you come to feed the cat...

I'm afraid I have a bit of a confession to make. The cruise to Norway sounded too good to miss so I snuck out last night while you were asleep and swapped places with Audrey. I didn't think she'd mind too much because she'll have so much fun with you while we're gone. Don't worry, she's fine, but you might want to let her out the wardrobe now—she's probably getting a bit hungry. I'll be sure to look after Mum and Dad and bring them back safe. Don't try and come after us though... I might get into one of my robot rages!

See you when we get back,

Love Awesome xx

P.S. Happy knitting!

Audrey read it through three times, getting crosser and crosser. *I'll be sure to look after Mum and Dad and bring them back safe.* As if Evil Techno-Twit wasn't the reason they were in danger in the first place.

"Huh!" she steamed. "Robot rage? You should try some Audrey anger. See you how you like that!"

Mr Windybags ran for cover as she reached full-on shouting level. "I HATE YOU," she yelled, shaking her fist at the letter as if it was a real person. Or a machine pretending to be a real person. "We should have taken you back to Professor Droyde's when we had the chance. We should have turned around the minute that stupid song came on the radio."

Audrey jumped at the sound of a key turning in the lock, her anger disappearing in a flood of relief. Grandad! He barely made it through the door before she threw her arms round his waist and started sobbing into his stripy pyjama top.

"Hey, come on, pet," he wheezed, out of breath from running. He ruffled her hair. "No more crying. It'll take more than a pesky robot to ruin *my* granddaughter's holiday. Come on, we can still catch them if we…" And then he stopped, taking his hand away from her hair and stepping backwards.

"Wait a minute." His voice was suddenly thick with suspicion. "How do I know you're the real Audrey?"

"What?" Audrey stared back at him, feeling stung. "Of course it's me, Grandad."

He started to smile but then seemed to think better of it. The distrustful frown was back. "Hmm. That's probably what *she'd* say too. I'm sorry, but I need to be sure this isn't some cunning robot trick to try and get me to kidnap my own flesh and blood."

"Of course it's not. You can't kidnap *me* because I'm already here. *Awful's* the one we want."

"Ah now then, I can tell you're not who you say you are because the *real* Audrey calls you Awesome. Hah! Gotcha!"

Audrey felt like her insides were being sucked out of her. "Please, Grandad. You *know* it's me. I changed her name because she's not Awesome after all. She doesn't deserve a name like that. And besides, she was there in the minibus when we chose it. So if I really was her, I'd know what the real me called me... I mean *she'd* know what the real her..."

She trailed off, too tangled up in her own sentence to carry on, and handed him the letter instead. "Look. You can go and see for yourself. There's no one in the wardrobe anymore. I managed to push it over and climb out the back." She paused again. "Unless you think I faked that too? Come on Grandad, please. If we don't hurry up and get to Southampton it'll be too late to stop her."

Grandad was wavering. She could see how much he wanted to believe her.

"I know!" said Audrey. "Your favourite colour's orange. And you secretly feed your Brussels sprouts to Mr Windybags at Christmas dinner."

"True and true," he agreed. "But Professor Droyde made a copy of all Audrey's memories in that scanner whatsit, so both of you would know that."

Audrey thought again. "Look," she said, holding out her left hand. "There's the mark where Mr Windybags scratched me last week. You remember, I was trying to put him in that knitted fart-catcher you made for him. And that was *after* we'd been to

Professor Droyde's so there's no way Awful would have a matching scratch too."

Grandad let out a huge sigh of relief. "You're right. You're absolutely right. I'm so sorry, pet, but I had to be sure." He gave her a quick hug and scooped Mrs Orr's car keys off the radiator shelf. "Let's go catch ourselves a rebel robot. To the Katmobile!" he cried.

9

Quite Possibly the Slowest Car Chase Ever

No wonder Audrey's parents had chosen to take Dad's car to Southampton—the Katmobile was already struggling by the time they reached Exeter. She was too old and rickety for long-distance robot-chases. Her exhaust pipe rattled and popped like it might fly off at any moment and there was an alarming noise coming from the engine. *We should have borrowed the minibus from Grandad's work again*, thought Audrey. She was sure the old ladies wouldn't have minded—they could have come along for the ride too if they wanted. A bit of extra company and a few handbags full of sucky mints and toffees would have been a good distraction from the dark thoughts whirling round her brain.

"Come on girl, you can do it," said Grandad, coaxing the spluttering car up yet another hill. Audrey caught a distant glimpse of the sea, twinkling through his window, and swallowed hard. Once that ship sailed, it would be too late.

"That's it. Almost at the top now." Grandad patted the dashboard, as if the Katmobile were a living creature with feelings. "And maybe a *little* bit faster on the way down, if you can manage it?" He turned to Audrey. "Don't worry, pet, there's still plenty of time." But even as the words were leaving his mouth, a tractor pulled out of a side road right in front of them. And not just any tractor—it was the most decrepit, dawdling tractor in the entire history of farming transport. If it went any slower, it would be going backwards.

Audrey bit her lip and switched on the radio to try and keep their spirits up. But thanks to the poor reception (and Grandad's yellow knitted aerial warmer), the only thing playing was a horrible static-y growl. Still, at least that was better than

Terence and the Machines. She *never* wanted to hear that song again.

"Do you think Awful was always evil?" she asked Grandad, rummaging around in the glove compartment for one of Mum's less tragic cassette tapes. The Katmobile was so ancient it didn't even have a CD player. "Or do you think it was the 'The Robot Rage' song that sent her crazy?"

"Oh I'm not sure she's *evil*," said Grandad, who always thought the best of everyone. Even nasty granddaughter-drugging machines with super-suction hands. "She's just badly wired. And that song seems to trigger something in her programming which makes her act out of character."

"But she locked me in the wardrobe," Audrey protested. "She stole my pyjamas and she *drugged* me." If that wasn't evil, then what was?

"True enough," admitted Grandad. "But she also left a note telling me where to find you. She wanted to make sure you were safe."

Audrey pulled out a copy of Abba's 'Greatest Hits'. That was about as good as Mrs Orr's tape collection got. "So you don't think she'll hurt Mum and Dad?"

"Of course not, pet," said Grandad. "She wants to go on holiday with them, that's all. As long as we get to her before she hears that song again, then everything—and everyone—should be absolutely fine. I'll have the professor sort out her programming and we'll be good to go. No real harm done apart from a broken wardrobe, and I'll have that all fixed up by the time you get back."

Audrey closed her eyes and gripped onto the door handle as Grandad attempted to overtake the tractor. The whole car shook and shuddered with the effort.

"Hah!" he cheered as they spluttered past. "Eat my dust, tractor man. I've got a boat to catch." He patted Audrey's knee. "Trust me, this time tomorrow you'll be a-snoozing and cruising in the lap of luxury, wondering what all the fuss was about."

Audrey hoped he was right. She pressed play and let the cheerful seventies music wash over her. *Yes, this time tomorrow,* she told herself, *I'll be in the middle of the North Sea without a care in the world. And Awful will be back to being her old Awesome self again. This time tomorrow…*

She woke with a start as Grandad swung the car into the *Scandinavian Cruises* VIP car park. "We're here," he said, pulling into an empty space between a brand new Jag and a Rolls Royce.

"We're here," Audrey echoed, gasping with wonder at the enormous, gleaming ship up ahead. It was bigger and brighter and better than anything she could have imagined. A hundred times more impressive than the laminated picture Mrs Orr had stuck to the fridge door. "Wow," she added, forgetting for a moment that finding the ship was the easy bit. Finding Awful and persuading her to trade places was where things got trickier. "Wow, wow and double wow."

"She's quite something, isn't she?" said Grandad, undoing his seat belt. "So let's go and sort out that rebel robot of yours and get you on board where you belong."

A grumpy, red-faced man in a high-visibility vest

stormed up to the car as they climbed out. "Excuse me, sir, you can't leave that here you know." He pointed to the Katmobile as if she was something yucky on the bottom of his shoe. "This is a VIP parking area for our VIP clients. That's Diamond class guests only."

Grandad pushed back his shoulders and lifted his nose in the air. "And how do you know *we're* not Diamond class?" he demanded haughtily, despite the fact that he was stood there in a pair of old jeans, a stripy pyjama top and mismatched shoes. Audrey hadn't even noticed his feet until now but the black leather lace up and bright green trainer combination didn't really say 'VIP' so much as 'dressed in the dark' or 'stark raving mad'.

The man looked doubtful but had the good grace to blush an even deeper red. "Ah. Yes. Sorry, sir. I was looking at the rust patches and that knitted 'thing' you're sporting on the aerial. To be honest, we don't get a lot of those in Diamond class." He peered in at the stripy seat covers and wrinkled up his nose. "If you'd just like to show me your boarding papers, I'll have the porter transfer your luggage over to the VIP embarkation lounge for you."

"Our papers?" said Grandad, patting his pyjama top as if he couldn't remember which of his invisible pockets he'd stowed them in.

"Yes, sir, that's right. If you wouldn't mind…"

"Goodness me!" Grandad pointed back towards the road with a look of wide-eyed astonishment. "Unless I'm very much mistaken, that looks like royalty arriving over there."

"Royalty? But we're not expecting anyone…" The man smoothed down his hair and spun round to see.

"Quick," hissed Grandad, grabbing Audrey by the shoulder and propelling her across the car park. "Run!"

They raced towards the main building, followed by furious shouting from behind.

"Oi, you! Come back. You can't leave that old banger here. It's against regulations. We need that space for *important* people."

"No one's more important than my granddaughter, and it's an emergency," Grandad yelled back, as he swerved to avoid a smug-looking older couple in matching designer tracksuits. The lady's jewel-encrusted earrings were so long they brushed against her shoulders when she walked.

"Well, really," she sniffed. "Scandinavian Cruise standards must be slipping. It seems they'll let *anyone* in Diamond class these days."

"Absolutely shocking," agreed Grandad in his fake posh voice, as he raced on past. "Rather like your dress sense. One sees nicer clothes at the car boot sale…"

Audrey let out a splutter of laughter as she ran.

"You'd better move that hideous heap of metal," yelled the parking guy, "or I'll… or I'll…" He stopped, as if he didn't really know what came next. Perhaps no one had ever dared park an orange rust bucket in his special diamond space before. "I mean it, mister… You come back here now."

Grandad leapt over the low metal barrier at the edge of the car park with a wild whoop. "Hasta la vista, baby!" he shouted back. "I've always wanted to say that," he added, grinning from ear to ear. "Never thought I'd be running through a cruise terminal in my pyjama top when I did, but hey, life's full of surprises."

"Look," said Audrey, pointing to the long line of holidaymakers snaking their way to the building marked 'Scandinavian Cruises: Standard Class Embarkation'. "There they are!" She was so pleased to see her parents safe and sound, she thought she might cry. And then she saw Awful, fake-laughing at something Dad was saying, and the soft mushy feelings turned to ice.

"See!" Grandad let out another wild whoop of triumph, flinging his arms up in a double-fisted victory air-punch. "I told you we'd make it. I feel like the hero in *Bad Grandad: Rock on Rocking Chair.*" He pushed his glasses up his nose with both index fingers, just like his film hero, and grinned some more. "Now to whisk that mis-wired imposter *out* of line, and sneak you *in*, without anyone noticing.

"Okay," agreed Audrey. "How are we going to do that?"

"Well," said Grandad. "We could always... Erm... " His grin faded and his shoulders sagged. "I'll think of something. Don't you worry."

10

Prince Whats-his-name to the Rescue

Grandad's 'something' turned out to be a crazy half-baked plan that was more full of holes than the knitted colander he'd made Mrs Orr for her birthday. But it was the only plan they had.

"Excuse me, please. Sorry!" They crept along the edge of the queue for luggage check-in, apologising to everyone as they went. "We're not pushing in, honestly. Just had to duck out for a last minute toilet trip…"

Audrey could see Mum and Dad clearly now—they were almost at the Baggage Drop. And she could *hear* them even more clearly. In fact, half of Southampton could probably hear them. Dad was singing his 'Happy Free Food to me' song, getting more excited—and tuneless—with each passing line, and Mum was practising Norwegian at the top of her voice. As for Awful, she was edging away from the pair of them, ashamed to be seen in public with such an embarrassing pair of humans.

"Perfect," whispered Grandad. "We've got her right where we want her." He gave Audrey the thumbs up and pulled half a ball of extra chunky orange wool out of his bulging jeans pocket. He always carried some with him—a different colour stowed away in every outfit—in case he needed it in an emergency. And now that emergency had finally arrived. He worked quickly, twisting and doubling up the wool for more strength and then looping it into a perfect lasso.

"You slip in and take her place the second I give the signal," he told Audrey. "I'll take care of everything else. You just need to get yourself on board that boat and have a fantastic time. Got it?"

"Yes, Grandad." She pushed herself up onto her tiptoes and planted a big kiss on his cheek. "Thank you," she said, "for everything. You're the best."

He gave her a mock salute. "All in a day's work for Bad Grandad! Now then. Are you ready to spot some more imaginary members of the royal family?"

"Ready."

Grandad took a deep breath and moved into position. "Look at that," he yelled at the top of his voice. "It's Prince Whats-his-name on board *The Scandinavian Queen!*"

There was a brief blur of orange whipping through the air as everyone turned their attention to the ship, jostling each other for a better view of his royal princeliness. Dad stopped singing, Mum stopped asking for pickled herrings in Norwegian, and Awful disappeared out of sight without so much as a cry. It all happened so quickly.

Audrey slipped into place behind her parents and pointed to the ship. "Yes! That's him up on the top deck. With the ginger hair and one of the Queen's corgis." Out of the corner of her eye she could see Grandad tugging Awful back across the VIP car park towards the Katmobile, his hand clamped across her mouth to keep her from screaming out. He'd done it! Just so long as no one reported him to the police as a suspected kidnapper…

Luckily, no one else seemed to have noticed. They were all too busy staring at the top deck of the ship, hoping for a glimpse of the imaginary prince.

"Yes," cried a shrill lady in a pink 'I ♥ CRUISING' baseball cap. "I see him too."

"Are you sure?" asked Mrs Orr, squinting into the morning sun. "That looks more like a crew member and a seagull to me." She turned to Audrey. "Those patches must be working their magic on your lazy eye if you can see him from this distance. I'll have to order some more. Don't you think, Pooh-pooh?"

Oh no. Not more patches, thought Audrey, although somehow the prospect didn't upset her *quite* as much as it might have done. Being stared at and teased by the Year 6 boys wasn't a nice feeling, but it wasn't as bad as having your family stolen away by an evil machine. Nothing was as bad as that.

"Come on, stop gawping and hurry up," said Mr Orr, not really listening. "I'm sure the prince and his seagull are both lovely but some of us are waiting for our breakfast."

Mrs Orr tutted and sighed, picking absentmindedly at Audrey's dirty t-shirt with her fingernail. "It's always food with you, isn't it, Pooh-pooh? Food and feet. Don't you ever think about anything else?" She leaned in closer to the offending t-shirt for a motherly sniff. "Yuck. Smells like... fish... and dirty washing."

"Ah. Yes," said Audrey. *Oops.* Grandad's genius daughter-swapping plan hadn't gone as far as swapping outfits. Not that there'd have been time anyway.

"I could have sworn you were wearing that nice new top when we left this morning," Mrs Orr went on. "And that skirt I bought last week."

Audrey gulped. "Yes. I was. Only..."

"Must have run off with that mysteriously vanishing scarf of yours," joked Mr Orr, shooting Audrey a sly wink.

"For the last time, it didn't just vanish," said his wife. "*Someone* must have moved it." And with that she launched into a ten minute rant about the impossibility of clothing disappearing of its own accord, and husbands who left the toilet seat up in the middle of the night and never remembered to put the rubbish out before they went to work.

"Huh. Well at least I don't run around coating everything in plastic," countered Mr Orr. Audrey's parents *loved* a good argument. Almost as much as they loved each other. Dad pulled a laminated shopping list out of his pocket and held it up as evidence. "What next? Laminated loo roll?"

Normally Audrey would have been embarrassed by their noisy bickering. But not today. She was so pleased to see them again, to be back where she belonged, that she smiled and left them to it. She smiled all the way through Baggage Check-In and Passport Control. She smiled for the camera at the Photo ID desk and was still smiling when they finally reached the ship. She even joined in with a few verses of Dad's song, until the lady in the pink baseball cap patted Mr Orr on the shoulder and asked them to stop.

"I don't mind a bit of tuneless wailing, myself," she said. "But we need to consider the royal ears."

11

All Aboard

"Welcome aboard *The Scandinavian Queen*," said the official welcoming lady, with an official welcoming smile. She scanned their ID cards and handed Audrey a travel pack.

"Ooh, has it got sweets in it?" asked Mr Orr hopefully. "Do I get one?"

"Yes. There are sweets and no, you can't have one," said the lady. "They're only for our younger guests, I'm afraid."

Audrey smiled back. "Thank you very much."

"*Tusen takk*, you mean," piped up Mrs Orr. "Like we practised in the car. Remember? After I won Eye Spy for the fifth time in a row…"

"Hmm," said Audrey, who hadn't actually been there. What else might she have missed? Hopefully nothing too important… just the usual car game squabbles.

"But you cheated," Mr Orr grumbled. "You can't do words in a foreign language and expect us to guess them… How was I supposed to know that 'car' is '*bil*' in Norwegian?"

"Don't worry," said the Welcome Lady. Her smile was getting a little less smiley round the edges as the queue started to build up behind the Orrs. "All the crew speak excellent English." She waved them forwards, but Mr Orr wasn't finished yet.

"You mean to say I've spent the whole week practising how to ask for pancakes and fungal cream for *nothing*?"

The lady shot him a strange look—half-puzzled, half-disgusted—before hurrying him on with a brisk wave of her hand. "Do have a pleasant trip, sir. And you, madame."

"Good luck," she whispered to Audrey. "There's a pair of headphones in your welcome pack if you need them…"

If Audrey had any doubts about whether it had all been worth it—the lies, the deceit, the not-so-high-speed car chase through the mean streets of Devon and Dorset—they vanished the moment she stepped on board. *The Scandinavian Queen* was even more impressive on the inside than it was on the outside. Everywhere she looked there were gleaming white walls with mirrored panels and expensive works of art, sparkling crystal lights hanging down from the ceiling, and huge picture windows with the blue sea gleaming beyond. Soft piano music drifted down from hidden speakers and the carpets were so thick and luxurious it felt like walking on air.

She glanced through the portside windows as they passed, keeping a lookout for Grandad. Not that she *wanted* to see him, of course. He'd be long gone by now, hopefully, assuming he hadn't been arrested for kidnapping, or wrestled to the ground by angry men in high-vis vests. But her lazy eye was being its usual lazy self, and the VIP car park was too far away and blurry to see properly. There were no sirens though, which was a good sign. And no blue flashing lights. *He'll be fine*, she told herself firmly. Awful might be awful but she was no match for Bad Grandad and his orange lasso. Besides, she couldn't get on the boat now if she tried—not without a passport and ticket—so it was all over for the robot rebellion. It was time to forget about terrible techno-twins, Audrey decided, and get on with having the time of her life, Family Orr style:

Happy cruise time for me, she sang under her breath, drinking in her majestic surroundings.

Happy cruise time for me,

Happy cruise time with my family,

No more robots for me.

"Come on," said Mr Orr. "The sooner we get to our cabin, the sooner we can hit the free food. There's a special embarkation buffet on Deck 14 with my name on it."

"What, the Pooh-pooh buffet?" joked Mrs Orr. "That's not a very appetising name for a meal, is it? Not sure anyone will want to try the sausages…"

Audrey giggled, despite herself. Embarrassing as her parents were, at least no one could accuse them of being boring.

"Ah, well," said Mr Orr. "That's because I've changed my name." He shook Audrey's hand. "Hello, nice to meet you. I'm Mr Pizza-Pasta-Sushi-Soup-Curry-Steak-Salad. It's a bit of a mouthful, I know, so do feel free to leave out the Salad part. I certainly intend to!"

"Honestly. Do try and behave yourself in public, Pooh-pooh," scolded Mrs Orr, but she was grinning even as she said it. "And if you're going to use your formal title at least make sure you get it right. I think you'll find it's Pizza-Pasta-Sushi-Soup-Curry-Steak-*Chips*-Salad. After your grandfather, I believe."

Audrey followed them, still giggling, to the lift, where a peculiar-looking man in a wide-brimmed cowboy hat and fake ginger moustache and beard stood staring. The tips of his moustache reached all the way up to his ears and there was a stray stick-on eyebrow peeking out from behind his glasses. A pair of glasses that didn't actually have any glass in them—just empty black frames. The man backed away slowly, as if the strange family sense of humour might somehow be catching, and then turned on his heel and fled away down the gleaming corridor.

"Funny-looking chap," observed Mr Orr, pressing the lift call button. "Did you see that bandage round his leg?"

"Hmm. I guess you get all sorts on a big ship like this," Mrs Orr murmured, her face buried in her handbag. Tissues and chewed biros flew out as she fumbled for her knitted Viking hat. "Still," she announced, pulling the woollen monstrosity all the way down to her eyes. She didn't seem to have noticed it was back-to-front. "At least *some* of us know how to dress for a Norwegian cruise."

The first thing Mrs Orr did when they were reunited with their luggage at the cabin, was get the laminated signs out of her suitcase. Along with a poster tube and three packs of sticky tack.

"I don't care what Ms English-Speaking-Crew says," she muttered to herself. "I promised the school this would be an educational trip and that's what it's going to be." With that she stuck a '*lugar*' (cabin) sign on the outside of their door, a '*toalett*' one on the inside lid of the toilet, and a '*televisjon*' one slap bang in the middle of the screen. Then she unrolled a giant geographical poster of Norway, hopped up onto the bed with her shoes still on, and stuck it to the ceiling.

Mr Orr, meanwhile, was busy arranging his foot cream collection along the gleaming bathroom shelf, humming under his breath. Audrey unpacked her clothes, tipped out the contents of her welcome pack, and wolfed down all four packets of sweets while no one was looking. Her three o'clock in the morning cookies seemed a very long time ago and her stomach was starting to rumble. And after that, for want of anything better to do, she pulled open the sliding door and stepped out onto the balcony, breathing in the fresh sea air.

It was hard to believe she was actually here, after everything that had happened. But there was no mistaking the warm sun on her skin, the salty tang of the sea in her nostrils, and the squawk of seagulls circling overheard. It was all so beautiful... so perfect... and that was before they'd even left England!

The lady on the next balcony along waved her glossy magazine at Audrey and smiled. Audrey waved back, the stress of her madcap morning finally beginning to melt away. The next-door neighbour on the other side was out enjoying the morning sun too. But he must have boarded earlier than the Orrs because he was already dozing in his chair, an open book resting on his chest like a sleeping baby. And down on the balcony below... Huh! It was the peculiar man in the cowboy hat!

Mum was right, Audrey decided, as she watched him rubbing the back of his bandaged leg against one of the chairs, like Mr Windybags scratching his back on the edge of the sofa. You really did get all sorts on a cruise. Cowboy Man's oversized headwear and giant ginger beard made *her* family look positively normal! Well, *slightly* more normal. Mrs Orr was still sporting her Viking hat but at least she didn't have it on back-to-front anymore.

The man was talking on his mobile phone, waving his free hand around like someone conducting an orchestra. Audrey leaned over the railing to try and listen in, curious to know if he *sounded* like a cowboy too. But there were too many other noises going on around her: the snoring from next door's balcony; seagulls calling to each other overhead; Dad's increasingly loud humming… She cupped her hands behind her ears and leaned over a bit further.

"Audrey Orr!" came Mum's calm-shattering scream from behind. "Get away from there before you fall!"

The snorer next door jolted awake with a snort, his book crashing to the floor, while Audrey flew backwards in shock, smashing into the table and chairs with an almighty clatter. She didn't see what happened to the man below—she just saw his mobile phone sailing out towards the water in a graceful arc, like a shiny black stone. *Oops!* she thought. *Sorry Mr Cowboy!*

"Honestly," said Mrs Orr, helping her back up onto her feet. "You've been acting very strangely today, what with that business in the car about machines taking over the world, and changing your outfit while no one's looking. And now I find you dangling headfirst off the balcony. If you fall and break your legs it'll spoil the holiday for everyone."

"Yes, Mum," said Audrey. "Sorry. It won't happen again."

"Good." Mrs Orr's expression softened. "Because from now on I intend to enjoy every single minute, starting with that Welcome Buffet on Deck 14. I think it's got *all* our names on it! Come on, Mr Pizza-Pasta-Sushi-Soup-Curry-Steak-Chips-Salad-Guzzlyguts," she called to Mr Orr. "Breakfast time."

For the next hour or so, Audrey forgot all about the clownish cowboy and his lost mobile phone. She was too busy eating. And drinking. And eating some more… Late breakfast ran seamlessly into brunch, which turned into early lunch as the Orrs moved from the buffet to the drinks fountain, with a quick stop for burgers at the poolside barbecue, then back to the buffet again. She forgot about Awful and eye patches and poor old Grandad… she forgot about everything. Until they went out onto the observation deck to watch the boat leave, that was.

"Good heavens," shrieked a tall, thin lady in a jewelled bikini, waving her empty cocktail glass around. "I think I'd better lay off the free drinks. I could have sworn I just saw a girl climbing up the side of the ship!"

12

She's Behind You...

If it was humanly possible to look over both shoulders at once, that's what Audrey would have spent the rest of the day doing.

I knew it, she thought bitterly, as the huge ship eased itself out of port. *I knew it was too good to be true.* Everyone around her was waving and cheering as if they didn't have a care in the world. As if the hiccupping lady in the bikini hadn't just announced the arrival of an unstoppable robot, slap bang in the middle of all their fun. But Audrey knew her holiday was as good as over. Awful was coming for her. She must have given Grandad the slip and come back for round two. And she didn't need a passport or a photo

ID card with suction hands and feet at her disposal. *Of course she didn't!* Audrey cursed herself for not realising that sooner. All Awful had to do was nip up the side of the boat while no one was looking, and *bingo!*

Audrey glanced round nervously, trying to work out which direction she'd be coming from. Any minute now there'd be a sharp crack against her skull or a karate chop to the back of the neck and *boom!* That would be it. If she was lucky, she'd wake up locked in a cupboard for the rest of the cruise. And if she wasn't, she'd probably wake up at the bottom of the sea. Only there wouldn't be much waking up to be done by then.

"Are you alright, darling?" asked Mrs Orr. "You've gone awfully pale, all of a sudden."

Audrey ran through the list of suitable lies in her head. She could claim it was tiredness, or seasickness, or too many slices of cheesecake on top of her pizza, curry, chips and burger feasting. But she decided against all of them. It was time she started telling the truth.

"Mum. Dad…" Actually she *was* feeling sick now, but it was nothing to do with the sea. "There's something I need to tell you."

"It's alright, sweetheart." Mrs Orr patted her arm. "I already know."

"You do?" said Mr Orr, looking from one to the other in confusion.

"You do?" Audrey echoed. Had she somehow wormed the truth out of Grandad and been playing along ever since? Or had Awful given the game away on the car journey? No, that didn't make any sense. Mum wouldn't have been waiting patiently in the boarding queue if she knew a robot had taken her daughter's place. She'd have been walloping the android imposter over the head with her suitcase until she begged to go back to Professor Droyde's.

"Of course," smiled Mrs Orr. "It's a mother's job to notice these things. I can always tell when your father's been at it too."

"You can?" said Mr Orr, looking increasingly worried.

What? Dad's been hiring robots too?

Mr Orr scratched his ear. "I'm sorry, love. I didn't realise you knew." He paused and scratched his other ear. "But just for the record, what are we actually talking about?"

"Robots," said Audrey.

"Sneaking dirty clothes back out of the washing basket to wear," said Mrs Orr. "There's a certain smell…"

"Oh," sighed Audrey. "Not robots then." She knew it was too good to be true. Of course Mum hadn't guessed about Awful. And Dad hadn't got himself a secret robot twin either. She took a deep breath and tried again. "No, Mum. You've got it all wrong."

"I don't think so." Mrs Orr leaned in for another t-shirt sniff and fanned her nose with her hands. "Yes, definite top notes of stale sweat and old socks. With the unmistakable scent of Eau de Tuna. Honestly, Audrey. If you didn't like the new skirt and top you should have said. I could have swapped them for something else. Why don't we go back to the cabin and you can change into something you *do* like?"

Audrey scanned the deck, searching the crowds for any sign of danger. Was she safer out here in the open, with hundreds of witnesses, or should she lie low in the hope that Awful wouldn't be able to track her down?

"Did you tell me which cabin we were staying in?" she asked. "I can't remember if we talked about it or not."

"It's number—" began Mr Orr.

"Shh." Audrey put a finger to her lips. "I don't need to know the number *now*. But did we talk about it this morning? In the car?"

"I don't think so," said Mrs Orr. "Why?" She placed a hand on Audrey's forehead as if she was checking her temperature. "Are you sure you're alright? You're behaving very strangely again."

"Perhaps we *should* go back to the cabin," Audrey agreed, checking round one last time. Still no sign of any raging robots. "I could do with a lie-down."

"What, now?" said Mr Orr. "Wouldn't you rather

wait until we've had afternoon tea in Café Karamell?" He patted his bulging shirt. "I'm starting to feel a bit peckish…"

Audrey shook her head. "Please. I just want to go to the cabin. Quickly. Before it's too late."

Mrs Orr took the 'quickly' bit very seriously indeed. She seemed to think Audrey's five course feast was about to put in a reappearance. "Out of the way," she yelled, flapping her arms like a windmill. "Queasy daughter coming through."

"Quickly and quietly, I meant," said Audrey under her breath.

Any rampaging robot within three hundred miles would have heard the Orr family barrelling towards their cabin. But there was no stopping Mum now. "Watch out," she roared at a passing crew member as they rounded the last corner. "She's going to blow!"

"There," said Mrs Orr, flinging the cabin door open with a cry of triumph. "We made it!"

Audrey peeled off the '*lugar*' sign as she went in, slipping it down behind the back of the sofa.

Otherwise they might as well announce their whereabouts on the ship's loudspeaker system: *Would all murderous machines please make their way to Room 7589, where Audrey Orr is waiting for you. Thank you.*

"Hurry up," she told her dad, who'd paused, halfway through shutting the door, to read the room service menu attached to the back. "Close it properly and make sure it's locked."

Mr Orr took no notice. "It says here you can't order a cream tea to your cabin until three o'clock." He checked his watch and sighed. "But that's ages away. Unless they mean Norwegian time."

"Please, Dad," Audrey begged. Awful might be scanning the corridors with her robot radar even now. "And keep your voice down." She couldn't let her find them—at least not until she'd had a chance to warn Mum and Dad. *They'd* know what to do. Wouldn't they?

"Don't worry about him," said Mrs Orr, bundling her into the bathroom. "You just get on with it." She lifted the toilet lid and seat up ready for splashdown.

"And don't worry about getting any on my *toalett* sign. It's all wipe clean. That's the beauty of laminating," she added, raising her voice to make sure Mr Orr could hear. "Even if *some* people don't appreciate it properly."

Audrey closed the lid back down again. "It's okay, Mum. I'm not going to be sick."

"Excellent," said Mr Orr. "Up to the café for early afternoon tea then."

"But there's something I need to tell you both. And it's nothing to do with washing baskets this time. I think you'd better sit down for this."

Her parents perched themselves on the end of the bed, looking puzzled.

"You think they might have left some chocolates on the pillows like they do in posh hotels," whispered Mr Orr. "I bet you get that in Diamond class."

"Mum. Dad. Erm…" Audrey barely knew where to begin. "What would you say if I told you I had a robot twin who looked and sounded exactly like me? Only she's evil and she wants to take over my life.

Well, she might not be *totally* evil, but she's definitely dangerous. And she'll stop at nothing to take my place on this holiday."

"A rogue robot, eh? Don't worry," said Mr Orr, as if it was all a joke. "I'll stun her with my fungal feet if she tries anything." He kicked his right leg up in the air. "Take that, Evil Audrey-bot!"

"I'm serious, Dad. She's already locked me in the wardrobe once today."

"Oh Audrey," said Mum. At least *she* looked properly worried. "I think you must be running a fever after all. Time to dig out the medicine box."

"No. I'm not sick. I'm scared. Please, you've got to believe me. That's the reason I'm not wearing my new skirt and top anymore. I never was. That was *her*."

Mrs Orr shook her head. "Let's get you some medicine, like I said. And then try and sleep it off. Hopefully you're just overtired. Or overexcited. Maybe sitting up half the night writing comic strips wasn't the best idea now, was it? Next thing we know, you'll be telling me she shredded Mr

Windybags!"

"What?" stammered Audrey. "You mean you *read* it? My Orz Um comic?"

"Not really," said Mrs Orr. "I happened to glance at it while I was tidying it away last night. That's all. It's good though—you've certainly got a very vivid imagination."

"P-P-POW!" Mr Orr fired off his other foot like a machine gun. "Take that you rascally robot. No one shreds *my* flatulent fleabag and gets away with it!"

"You read it," said Audrey again. "But Orz Um is private. It's only for me and Grandad."

Mrs Orr's face fell. "So it's okay for Grandad to read it," she sniffed, "but not us? I see."

"It's not like that… it's just…" but Audrey couldn't explain it without hurting their feelings, any more than she could convince them of the terrible danger heading their way. "This isn't comics anymore, Mum. This is real life. That lady who thought she saw a girl climbing up the side of the ship must have spotted Awful coming to get me."

Mrs Orr was already unscrewing the lid of the

brown medicine bottle. "That's enough of this nonsense. You'll feel better after a sleep."

"Or a trip to the café?" suggested Mr Orr. But then he caught sight of the expression on his wife's face. "Maybe a quick nap and *then* the café. How about that?"

13
Oh No She Isn't, Oh Yes She Is

Audrey swallowed her medicine and pretended to sleep, listening out for any sounds of techno-twin attack.

"I'm worried, Pooh-pooh," she heard her mum saying. "It's not like Audrey to make up stories."

"I'm sure it's nothing," answered her dad. "Nothing that a room service sandwich wouldn't fix, anyway."

"I'm being serious."

"So am I," he grumbled.

Mrs Orr let out a long sigh. "I know she's been finding it hard settling into a new school—her teacher told me there'd been another incident with children making jokes about her eye patch. But I didn't realise things were as bad as all *this*. She must have retreated into her own imaginary world to cope with it all. Oh, it breaks my heart."

It's not imaginary, Audrey wanted to shout. *I only wish it was.* Lonely lunch times and eye-patch jokes were the least of her worries now.

"Hmm," said Mr Orr. "Perhaps we should have another talk with her teacher when we get back if it's still an issue. Or make an appointment to see Mr Stickler."

No! Audrey stiffened. She couldn't let them talk to *him* about her behaviour on holiday. As far as the headmaster was concerned, she'd never even left school… And that's when it hit her. There *was* no robot double filling in for her in lessons because she was too busy stowing away on-board *The Scandinavian Queen*. Despite all their efforts—even after everything that had happened—Audrey was *still* going to get expelled. If she made it back alive, that was.

It took all of her self-control to carry on

'sleeping' after that. To keep from screaming out loud at the unfairness of it all. How had everything gone so wrong?

"Look, why don't we humour her for now?" suggested Mr Orr. "Let's go along with this robot story and hope she settles down again. There's no point upsetting her even more."

"I suppose," said Mrs Orr, although she didn't sound convinced. "Robot doubles indeed. Whatever next?"

Having her parents *pretend* to believe her wasn't ideal, but it was better than nothing. At least now Audrey didn't have to lie anymore. She spilled out the whole sorry story from start to finish as the family tucked into their room service cream tea that afternoon. Her mum and dad nodded their heads and smiled and tutted in all the right places but clearly didn't believe a word of it.

"Well," said Mr Orr. "Fancy that."

"Who'd have thought it?" said Mrs Orr. "A robot Audrey, eh? More jam, Pooh-pooh?"

"That's why we need to stay here," Audrey told them, firmly. "In the cabin, with the doors and windows locked. It's the safest place."

"Nonsense," snorted Mrs Orr. "It'll take more than an overgrown microwave on legs to ruin *my* holiday. It's taken me ten years to win this break and we're going to enjoy every single minute of it. Whether we like it or not."

"But you don't know how cunning she can be..." Audrey protested.

"Don't worry, darling. We won't let her hurt you. Will we, Pooh-pooh?"

Audrey tried coming at the problem from a different angle. Mum might not believe in robot twins, but she *definitely* believed in school. "What about Mr Stickler though? He'll expel me if I don't get off this boat and go home."

"Of course he won't. You really must stop worrying, Audrey. It's not healthy."

She gave it one last shot. "And what about

Grandad? What if Awful hurt him when she escaped? What if he's lying in the VIP car park in a pool of his own blood?" The man in the high-vis vest definitely wouldn't approve of that. *Oi, you. No bleeding to death in here unless you're Diamond class.*

Mrs Orr rolled her eyes at her husband and sighed. "I'm sure Grandad can look after himself," she said in a false, bright voice.

"We need to ring him and check he's okay."

Mrs Orr sighed again. "Alright. We'll give him a call when we get to Bergen. Happy now?"

No, thought Audrey. Of course she wasn't happy. She was terrified. But she nodded anyway. What choice did she have? "Just promise me you'll be careful," she pleaded. "Really careful. And don't let me out of your sight for a single second."

She stuck to her parents like glue for the rest of the day, assuming Awful was waiting to get her alone. She could feel her following them round the ship—lurking behind the mosaic pillars at the indoor swimming pool; crouching under the food-laden tables in the Thor Bistro; slinking through the shadows at the back of the basketball court. But every time she turned to see, there was no one there.

"You're quite safe, darling," Mrs Orr assured her over dinner. "Do try and relax."

"She's watching us," said Audrey, her skin prickling. "I can feel it."

"Have some more chocolate pudding," suggested Mr Orr, tucking into his second bowlful. "It's ever so tasty. Oh look, there's that funny cowboy fellow again. Ahoy there!" he called. "Oh no, wait, that's pirates isn't it? I mean yee-haw! Giddy up!"

"Don't encourage the man," Mrs Orr hissed. "I swear he's following us. Every time I look up, there he is."

Really? Audrey hadn't even noticed. She'd been too busy watching out for Awful.

"It's probably *me* he's been trailing," said Mr Orr. "Or my toes, rather. I'm quite a celebrity in the fungal-foot-blogging world, you know. I had four whole followers last time I checked."

"Oh great," sighed Mrs Orr. "So now we've got a runaway robot *and* a crazy toe-stalker trying to spoil our fun. The competition terms and conditions didn't mention anything about *them*. I've a good mind to complain."

"No need for that, dear, I'm sure he's harmless," said Mr Orr, signalling to the waiter to come back with the dessert trolley. For the fifth time. "Have a slice of that cheesecake instead. It's quite delicious."

Somehow Audrey made it all the way to bedtime without getting clobbered on the head or thrown overboard. She still couldn't shake the feeling that she was being watched—that Awful was following her—but maybe Mum was right. Maybe it had been the crazy cowboy man all along. And then a new, creepier thought struck her. What if they were working together? What if Awful had recruited him to spy on their movements, while she got on with plotting and scheming and preparing to strike?

She barely slept a wink all night, straining her ears above the sound of Dad's snoring for signs of a robotic break-in. If Awful could modify herself a set of suction hands and feet, she could probably re-programme her nose to cut through double-glazed glass as well. But when morning eventually arrived the balcony door was still in one piece. And so was Audrey.

There was no sign of Awful at breakfast. Or at second breakfast. Not even at the third. She didn't creep into the cinema and spirit Audrey away in the darkness, or jump out and hit her over the head with a wooden spoon during the baking demonstration on Deck 12. Four lunches came and went without incident—other than Mr Orr arguing with a toddler over the last strawberry jelly—and slowly but surely Audrey began to relax.

There was a scary five minutes at the tropical fun pool that afternoon, when 'The Robot Rage' came blaring out of the speakers at top volume, but still no sign of her techno-twin. No red eyes glinting in the crowds; no metallic voice chanting in the background; and no sign of anyone eating up an entire poolside burger grill in a post-robot-rage burst of hunger. Nothing but a distant glimpse of ginger beard and cowboy hat, and the gentle 'pop' of Mr Orr's trouser button as he lowered himself onto a lounger to sleep off his entire bodyweight in hot dogs and quarter pounders.

"You see," said Mrs Orr, as they sat outside on the balcony that evening, resting after a hard day's eating. "That can't have been your robot friend, climbing up the outside of the boat, otherwise we'd have seen her by now. So stop worrying and give me a smile. Just think, when we wake up tomorrow we'll be in Bergen. That's when the holiday *really* begins."

"And that's when we ring Grandad." Audrey imagined him laughing down at the phone at her. *No, pet, of course she didn't give me the slip. She's right here with me now, doing your homework. The professor fixed her up and she's as good as new.* If only.

"Yes, darling. We'll ring Grandad if you want. And then we're going to forget all about runaway robots and enjoy our day in the city. Agreed?"

Audrey nodded. Perhaps it hadn't been Awful scampering up the side of the ship after all. Maybe the lady in the jewelled bikini really *had* imagined the whole thing. And maybe, just maybe, everything was going to be okay.

"Aaaarrgghhh!" No sooner had Audrey let her guard down than the quiet was shattered by a blood-curdling scream from Mr Orr. "No!" he cried, lurching to his feet with a pale face and wild, staring eyes. "No, no, no!"

"What is it, Pooh-pooh? What's wrong?"

But Audrey already knew the answer to that one. *It's Awful!* she thought, a cold wave of panic washing all the way up her body. *She's here!* Or at least she had been…

"What happened?" she asked Dad, scanning the balcony and empty cabin for a sign of her double-crossing double. "Where did she go?"

"Who?" replied Mr Orr, weakly, clutching at his chest as if he'd been shot. "What are you talking about?"

"Awful. She was just here. Wasn't she? I thought that's why you were screaming."

"You mean she's *real?*" gasped Mrs Orr. "What's she done to you, Pooh-pooh? Are you hurt? Talk to me."

"No, no, it's nothing like that," said Mr Orr, finally recovering his wits. "I haven't seen any runaway robots."

Thank goodness, thought Audrey, shaking all over with shock and adrenaline.

"Thank goodness for that," echoed Mrs Orr.

"But it *is* awful all the same," Mr Orr insisted. "I realised we've been on this boat for the best part of two days and we *still* haven't tried out the Soft-Scoop-2000! Oh, how could I have let this happen?"

14

Hello, Is Anybody There?

Mrs Orr's excitement was infectious.

"We're here!" she shrieked, grabbing Audrey by the shoulders and dancing her across the cabin.

"We're here!" she screamed, grabbing Mr Orr by the waist and prancing him round the bed.

"We're here!" she squealed, sliding open the balcony door and waving her guidebook at the blue Bergen sky.

"Better get a move on with breakfast then," said Mr Orr. "I'll take my rucksack with me and fill it up for lunch."

"Try and be discreet, Pooh-pooh," said Mrs Orr, putting on her green knitted Viking helmet.

"Of course," he said. "Discretion is my middle name."

Five minutes later, he was waving his bulging rucksack over his head and shouting down the length of the hot food counter. "Kat! I can't fit any more sausages in on top of all those blueberry muffins. Have you got any room in your handbag?"

"Discreetly, I said," Mrs Orr hissed back.

Audrey blushed. "Sorry," she told the serving assistant, who was watching the whole exchange in amusement. "My dad's got rather a big appetite. And a big mouth to match."

"Don't worry," she said. "I've seen it all before. I once caught a woman sneaking bacon into her shoes when she thought no one was looking." She shook her head. "Sea air and free food does funny things to folks. Apparently, someone cleared out the whole of Café Karamell yesterday afternoon. Every single sandwich, bun, cake, muffin and scone in the entire place. Same story with the Soft-Scoop-2000 up on the sun deck. Not a single drop of ice cream left. Only about your age too. It's a wonder she didn't pop."

Audrey's red cheeks paled again. Someone her age with an uncontrollable craving for food? "W-what did she look like? Was it before or after they played 'The Robot Rage' at the swimming pool?"

"Oh, I don't know the details," said the lady. "I shouldn't think she's feeling very well this morning though!"

"No, probably not," agreed Audrey, staring down at her plate of pancakes and feeling rather sick herself. The old fear came flooding back through her veins with a vengeance. The sooner they got hold of Grandad and found out the truth, the better. It certainly *sounded* like Awful. But then why hadn't she made her move? Was she still waiting to get Audrey on her own? Or had she already got what she wanted—a place on the cruise instead of boring old school lessons?

"Come on, you two," said Mrs Orr, dragging them back to her table. "Hurry up and get that food down you. We don't want to keep Norway waiting."

It felt funny being on solid ground again after a full day and a half at sea. But it was a nice kind of funny. And Bergen was every bit as beautiful as it looked in the guidebook. Annoyingly short of telephone boxes, but beautiful all the same.

Mrs Orr led them along to Bryggen, the old waterfront with the colourful wooden warehouses that matched Audrey's new eye patch, humming over her breath as she went. Which was like humming *under* her breath but ten times louder.

"Okay," she said after what felt like a *lot* of humming. "Educational lesson for the day. Who knows what tune that was?"

"Ooh, me," said Mr Orr, putting up his hand as if Mrs Orr was his schoolteacher instead of his wife. "It's the music from the foot cream advert. I love that one." And with that he was off, singing away at the top of his voice:

"Have you got fungus on your feet,

An itch between your toes?
A tube of Toe-tal Health Complete
Will soon make sure it goes."

Passers-by turned to stare. But for once, they weren't looking at Audrey's eye patch. One old man had his hands over his ears and a little girl in a pushchair started screaming.

"That's enough, Pooh-pooh," cut in Mrs Orr, as a lady on crutches hobbled up to them, pressing a coin into his hand.

"Oh no, I'm not a busker," Mr Orr explained. "My singing's quite free. My gift to the people of Bergen." He turned to his wife. "What's Norwegian for 'busking'?"

The lady nodded. "It's alright. I understand," she said in perfect English. "I'm paying you *not* to sing." She hobbled off again, leaving Mr Orr looking crestfallen.

"Never mind, dear," said Mrs Orr. "It wasn't the foot cream song anyway. It's 'Morning' by the famous Bergen composer, Edvard Grieg. We can go and visit his house later if there's time." She looked very pleased with herself. "There you go, Audrey, that's another educational tick in the box for Mr Stickler."

But Audrey didn't want to think about her headmaster—she was still looking for a telephone box. Maybe they didn't have them in Bergen anymore. "How are we going to ring Grandad if we can't find a phone?" she fretted.

Mrs Orr sighed. "Really, darling, you're worrying over nothing. If anything had happened to him we'd have heard by now. The police would have got a message to us somehow."

"Please, Mum. I won't be able to enjoy the day until I've spoken to him." She hadn't told her parents about the girl who'd cleaned out all the cakes and ice creams on the entire ship. Mrs Orr wouldn't believe it—because she didn't believe anything Audrey told her about Awful—and Mr Orr would probably just be jealous. *How come she's allowed to eat an entire café in one sitting and I'm not?* "You promised we'd call when we got to Bergen."

"I know I did," said Mrs Orr, "but I can't magic a telephone out of thin air, can I?"

"Maybe we could ask in there," suggested Audrey, pointing to a nearby souvenir shop. The window had a colourful display of patterned jumpers and painted bowls, with a row of Viking helmets hanging down from the top like bunting. "They might have a phone we could borrow if we're buying something... like a present for Grandad, to say thank you for looking after Mr Windybags." *And sorry for leaving you in the car park with a crazy robot*, she added silently. "What about that big troll in the middle, with the green trousers and sticky up hair. He even looks a bit like him, don't you think?"

Mrs Orr peered through the glass at the price tag and let out a low whistle. It wasn't 'Morning' by Edvard Grieg this time though—more like 'My Goodness That's a Lot of Money' by the You've Got To Be Kidding Sisters.

"Ooh, look," said Mr Orr, spotting the baker's shop next door. "Why don't we try that one, instead?" He pulled out his wallet in readiness and patted his stomach. "I know it's not long since breakfast but I should be able to squeeze in a cinnamon bun or three. Seeing as it's an emergency." He ducked into the shop before anyone could answer, sticking his head back out the door a few minutes later, wearing a big smile and a long cinnamon smudge down the front of his t-shirt.

"Sometimes fathers have to make sacrifices for their children," he said, licking his fingers. "And I'm pleased to say this is one of the tastiest sacrifices I've ever made." He pulled a face, as if he was working a stray lump of raisin out of his back teeth. "Ha! Gotcha! Oh yes, and the nice lady behind the counter says you're welcome to borrow her mobile, as a thank you to me for buying all her buns. But you'll have to do it in here where she can keep an eye on you."

He held the door open for Audrey and her mum, before heading back outside to finish off the rest of his second breakfast. "Say 'hello' to Grandad from me, won't you? And tell him to watch his shoes when he goes to feed Mr Windybags. Best to keep them firmly on his feet if he wants to avoid the *other* kind of thank you present."

"Thank you so much," said Mrs Orr, as the shop lady handed over a sugar-dusted smartphone. "I mean, *tusen takk*." She dialled the top number on her specially laminated 'International Dialling' card and moved over to the window, away from the counter. "It's ringing," she announced, although Audrey could hear that for herself.

Please pick up, Grandad, she prayed. *Please tell me you're okay. Tell me Awful is safely back in England. In lessons.*

The phone rang. And rang. "Hello," said Grandad's voice at last, sending giddy sparks of relief coursing through Audrey's body.

Thank goodness! "Can I talk to him?"

The answer, as it turned out, was 'no'.

"I'm sorry I can't come to the phone right now," Grandad went on. "I'm probably too busy knitting. Leave a message after the tone and I'll ring you back later. Cheerio."

"What? No! He's *got* to be there," said Audrey,

grabbing the phone out of her mum's hand and pressing it to her own ear. "It's me. Audrey. Please pick up, Grandad. I need to know you're alright. I need to know if Awful's with you. Pleeease, Graaaandddaaad!" she sobbed, begging him over and over until the phone was prised away from her clenched fingers.

"Sorry about that, Dad," said Mrs Orr, "a little misunderstanding at our end, that's all. Nothing to worry about. We're all fine and having a lovely holiday. See you next week." She ended the call with a loud sigh. "Honestly Audrey, there's no need to get in such a state. Whatever will the other customers think? I expect he just swapped shifts at work."

"No he hasn't," said Audrey, staring out the window at the pretty harbour scene as if it was something out of a horror movie. She didn't see the colourful buildings and sparkling water. She didn't see brilliant blue skies and mountains and happy holidaymakers strolling along in the sunshine. She just saw robots. Evil, raging, Grandad-bashing, cake-scoffing robots, intent on ruining everything.

"He's hurt. That's why he can't get to the phone. Oh, Mum," she said, sniffing into Mrs Orr's hand-stencilled 'I ♥ NORWAY MORE THAN CHIPS' t-shirt. "What if he's…" But she couldn't even finish the sentence. It was too awful.

Mrs Orr glanced over at the counter, to make sure the lady wasn't waiting for her phone, and ruffled Audrey's hair. "Don't cry, sweetheart. I'll try him at work quickly, just to set your mind at rest. You'll have to wait outside with Dad though. It's getting too busy in here."

"But *I* want to talk to him."

"And I want you to wait outside," said Mrs Orr, firmly. "Look at the state of you," she added, dabbing at Audrey's tear-stained cheeks. "We don't want you scaring the customers away after the lady's been so kind to us, do we?"

"But, but…"

But nothing. Audrey knew better than to argue with her mum once she'd made up her mind. She had to settle for watching through the window, hoping against hope that Mrs Orr's head nods and smiles meant she'd finally got hold of him. That he was okay.

"Well?" she demanded, once her mum had returned the phone and joined them outside. "What did he say? Did you get to speak to him? Is he alright?"

"Grandad's fine," Mrs Orr assured her. "He'd just taken on an extra morning shift, like I said. See, I told you there was nothing to worry about."

"Are you sure?" said Audrey. "And what about Awful? Did he say anything about her? Is she at school?"

Mrs Orr paused for a moment, as if she was having trouble remembering. "He said he couldn't talk for long, but to tell you that everything's okay. Couldn't be better. Yes, that's right. He said not to give Awful another second's thought and to enjoy your day out in Bergen."

"Really?"

"Really," repeated Mrs Orr. "*Now* can get we on with our holiday?"

"Yes," said Audrey. The evil robots disappeared

again, melting away like a bad dream, leaving her with a beautiful summer's day and a city full of waiting adventures. "Yes, yes, and double yes. Let's go!"

15

Say Cheese

With only eight hours on shore, Mrs Orr was determined to cram in as many sights as possible. And Mr Orr was determined to cram in as many breakfast buffet sausages and blueberry muffins as possible. He left a tell-tale trail of crumbs along the cobbled streets and steep alleyways of the old town, and lost half a sausage to a passing seagull down near the fish market. By the time they'd climbed to the top of the Rosenkrantz Tower and marched round the octagonal lake (and then retraced their steps, hunting for Mrs Orr's dropped Viking hat), his rucksack was looking decidedly less bulgy than before.

"There it is," said Audrey, finally spotting the green horned hat on top of a serious-looking statue. Someone must have put it there for safekeeping. "It quite suits him, don't you think?" She pulled her matching pink one out of her bag and posed for a photo next to her new stone friend.

"What about you, Kat?" asked Mr Orr. "Do you want to be in the next one with Audrey?"

But Mrs Orr was staring over his shoulder with a face like thunder.

"Look! There he is again."

"Who?" asked the others, in perfect unison.

"That creepy chap from the boat with the fake beard. I *knew* he was following us." Mrs Orr narrowed her eyes and pursed her lips. "He's not wearing his cowboy hat today but it's him, alright. I'm sure of it." She set off after him, picking up speed as she went.

"Hey, Kat, wait for us," said Mr Orr, fumbling with his camera case. "What are you going to do?"

"I'm going to find out what he's up to," she called back. "I don't like people spying on my family. And I *really* don't like fake beards. They look ridiculous and they make your chin all itchy."

"She's right," agreed Mr Orr. "I once went to a fancy dress party as Francis Drake. Itchiest night of my life."

They watched Mrs Orr storming towards her bearded victim. He was wearing an oversized black baseball cap this time, pulled down low over his face, and had swapped his fake glasses for mirrored shades. It was definitely him though—the bandaged leg was a dead giveaway.

"Do you *really* think he's one of your foot blog fans?" asked Audrey, stowing the Viking hats safely inside her bag as they trailed along behind. "I mean, you've only got four followers and one of them's Grandad." At least she knew he wasn't reporting back to Awful, whoever he was. He couldn't be, because Awful was safely back in England doing maths and spellings.

"Either that or he works for the travel magazine running the cruise competition," said Mr Orr, who'd obviously been giving the matter some thought. "He was jotting things down in a notebook when I saw him at breakfast this morning. Perhaps he's writing a feature article on us for their next edition."

Audrey giggled. "Well, this is his chance to get some very cross quotes from the lucky winner."

But the undercover journalist (if that's who he was) didn't seem very interested in talking to Mrs Orr. He was already off. Mrs Orr, meanwhile, had broken into a gallop behind him and was yelling at the top of her voice.

"Don't you run away from *me*, you beardy creep," she shouted. "Come back here and explain yourself!"

For a man with a bandaged leg, Beardy was surprisingly fast. Too fast for Mrs Orr, who lost him down one of the side streets and collapsed in a panting heap outside a 7-Eleven shop.

"Too... hot... to... run," she gasped as the others came to her rescue, hauling her back up onto her feet. "Need... a... drink." She patted Mr Orr's rucksack. "Maybe... a muffin too."

Mr Orr frowned. "Ah. Yes. Might be a slight

problem on the muffin front. It's hungry work exploring a new country, you know. Why don't we pop in here and get some fresh water and a bite to eat?"

They picnicked on bacon-wrapped hot dogs and a giant packet of *paprika potetgull*, which were the nicest crisps Audrey had ever eaten. She'd been too worried about Awful to appreciate her breakfast but she enjoyed every single bite of their late lunch. Especially the melty Norwegian chocolate they finished off with, washing the whole lot down with bottles of ice-cold water.

"Now," said Mrs Orr, looking at her watch. She seemed to have forgotten about the beardy man again. With any luck she'd scared him off for good. "We've got time for one more thing before we need to head back to the ship. What do you fancy, Audrey? Edvard Grieg's house? The aquarium? Or we could take the funicular railway up the mountain."

Audrey didn't have to think for long. They'd been to the National Marine Aquarium in Plymouth twice in the last month. And Grieg's house would probably set Mum off humming again. But a train up a mountain? That sounded like the perfect end to a perfect day…

And it was.

Almost.

><≶

The seven-minute ride up to the top of the Fløyen Mountain was surprisingly gentle. Mrs Orr spent the journey reading out loud from her Bergen guide book while Mr Orr slept off his lunch, his head lolling against the shoulder of the sporty-looking man next to him. Every few breaths he let out a soft snumble—half-snore, half-mumble—muttering something in his sleep about dinner reservations.

Audrey stared out the window at the passing trees, dreaming up a brand new adventure for Orz Um. One with a mysterious bearded spy who followed her round the city in disguise, then hid on top of the funicular carriage ready to leap on the laser-eyed hero when they reached the top.

"Mount Ulriken is the highest of the seven mountains in Bergen," Mrs Orr was saying. "But that's a cable car ride up to the top. And I don't like the way they swing in the wind..."

In her head, Audrey swapped the funicular for a cable car, imagining the box swaying under the weight of her bearded spy. She whipped up a bit of wind for good measure, almost blowing the fake beard off his face. Yes. He'd be so busy sticking his facial hair back on he wouldn't notice Orz Um hanging out the cable car window. He wouldn't spot her clambering out onto the narrow laddered roof behind him... until it was too late. *POW!*

"Oh look, we're there already," said Mrs Orr. "Wake up, Pooh-pooh. Wipe the dribble off that poor man's shoulder. It's time to go."

Audrey wished she'd brought her notebook and pencil with her to sketch out all her new ideas. But she'd had too much on her mind that morning to think about comic strips. She took a mental snapshot of Orz crawling up the side of the swaying cable car

as they walked up to the viewing platform, hoping to recreate the scene when she returned to her cabin later. It was funny, when she glanced back she could almost make out a real figure scrambling off the station roof. But then she blinked her eyes against the bright sunshine and the figure disappeared again.

The views from the top were stunning. Audrey and Mrs Orr posed for more Viking hat photos, with the city and the fjords spread out behind them, and Mr Orr snapped off a few scenic toe shots for his blog.

"Smile!" he said to his left foot. "Say cheese," he told the right.

"Cheese is the right word for it," said Mrs Orr, pinching her nose. "Put your socks back on, Pooh-pooh, you're scaring everyone away."

"But I need some more photos for my online slideshow. My fans will be expecting it…"

"Oh well, it's up to you, but I think I heard someone mention a waffle buffet up at the café," said Mrs Orr. "With ten different toppings to choose from."

Audrey had never seen anyone put their socks and shoes on so quickly. He didn't even stop to do up the laces.

"How about you and I stroll up to the shop and look for a present for Grandad while we're waiting?" said Mrs Orr. "I have a feeling Dad might be some time."

Audrey skipped along beside her, feeling decidedly cheerful. Awful was back where she belonged, Mum had scared off Mr Beardy, and her old worries about lazy eyes and sticker patches seemed a world away now. No one here cared what she looked like. And it's not as if she'd be wearing a patch for ever—it was only until her lazy eye caught up with the other one. Yes, even with one eye covered up, life looked sunny and bright all of a sudden, just like the view. It was funny how quickly things could change.

The Orrs must have picked a particularly busy time to visit the shop, unfortunately. It was heaving with sweaty tourists, so Audrey left her mum to it and headed back out into the sunshine to plan out

the next instalment of her Orz Um adventure. A laser eye shoot-out while dangling upside down from the bottom of the cable car maybe? That would be good.

"Audrey!"

Huh? That was strange. It sounded like someone calling her name. Stranger still, it sounded like Grandad. But that was impossible. "Over here, pet."

She stared around in confusion, trying to work out where the voice was coming from. Those trees over there?

"Please, Audrey, hurry."

She edged closer. Yes. It was definitely coming from the trees. But Mum had spoken to Grandad at work that morning—there's no way he could be lurking in the woods at the top of a Bergen mountain.

Unless she'd only been *pretending* to talk to him, to stop Audrey from worrying... *Of course! That's why Mum made me wait outside,* she realised. *She faked the whole thing!*

"It's Awful," said the voice. He sounded scared. "She's got me. I don't know how much longer I can hold on…"

Audrey forgot all about waiting for Mum and broke into a sprint.

"Don't worry, Grandad," she called back. "I'm coming!"

16

What Happens in Bergen, Stays in Bergen

Audrey followed the voice deeper into the trees, her mind racing. What could have happened to bring him all the way out here? *How* had he got here, come to that? Surely he and Awful couldn't *both* have stowed away on board *The Scandinavian Queen* without anyone noticing?

"Grandad?"

"Almost there, pet. I think I can see you."

"Well I can't see you." Audrey peeled up her special Bergen eye patch and peered into the shadows.

THWUMP! A hand slapped against her mouth.

SCHWOOMP! A foot caught her under the knee,

bringing her down with a soft thud, sending sparks of pain and panic careering through her whole body. What was happening?

Audrey tried to scream but the sticky hand was still clamped tight over her mouth. She couldn't bite her way out either—the fingers holding her jaw shut were too strong.

"Hooray, you found me!" said a voice from behind. Only it wasn't Grandad this time. It was Awful. "I *knew* you wouldn't be able to resist the 'grandfather in distress' routine," she crowed, slipping her other hand round Audrey's waist and hoisting her up into the air. She was one seriously strong robot now—another modification maybe? "You have to admit, it was a pretty good impression of him."

"Mmmhhhuuuhhhhmhhhummm," said Audrey, through a mouthful of hand. Thoughts and questions swarmed round her head like a cloud of killer bees: *Where are you taking me? What have I ever done to you? Where's Grandad? Why is your hand all sticky?* But mainly just *AAAARRRGGGHHHH!*

Help!

"Sorry, I can't understand a word you're saying," said Awful, cheerfully. "You'll have to wait until we're safely out of earshot." She picked up speed, zigzagging through the woods with precision skill. If Professor Droyde *had* given her a lazy eye to match Audrey's, it was a whole lot better at judging distances than the original version. She didn't smack into a single tree.

"There," she finally announced, dropping Audrey back down onto the ground. "That should do it." Audrey stared up at her techno-twin in sickened disbelief. She was wearing an almost identical outfit—denim shorts and a red t-shirt that looked suspiciously like the one Audrey had left folded up in the cabin wardrobe—and was grinning like a crazy person. Like a crazy robot, anyway.

"Why are you doing this?" Audrey asked, trying to keep the scared wobble out of her voice. "Where's Grandad?"

"Oh, he's fine. A couple of black eyes, maybe, and a sore head, but nothing a quick trip to

Southampton Accident and Emergency won't fix."

"You'd better be joking or…"

"Or what?" teased Awful. "You'll zap me with your laser eye?" Her grin got even wider. "It wasn't me anyway," she said. "It was that nutter in the bright yellow vest. They got into a fight about the Katmobile and I managed to slip away onto the boat. With this," she added proudly, holding up a familiar-looking length of extra chunky orange wool. "I thought it might come in useful." She hauled Audrey up onto her feet, removed her rucksack, and pushed her back against the trunk of a large tree. "Now, we can do this the easy way or the hard way."

Audrey was shaking so much she could hardly stay upright. But she didn't want Awful to see how terrified she was. "W-what's the easy way?"

"You stay there and do what you're told."

"Oh. I'll go with that one then." It didn't take a cunning robot genius to guess what Awful had planned for the orange wool if Audrey refused to co-operate. And however bad things seemed now, they'd be a whole lot worse if she ended up tied to a tree. There'd be no chance of escape then. "Y-you still haven't told me why you're doing this though," she added. "I mean, you wanted to come on holiday—I get that—but here you are. You *are* on holiday. And if you can sneak on and off the ship without anyone noticing, why can't we carry on as we are?" Audrey tried to drag her trembling lips into a smile. "That way everyone gets to enjoy the cruise." *And I can try and get hold of the professor to see about turning you off once and for all.* "Please, Awful. I mean, Awesome. Can't we go back to being friends?"

"We were never friends," Awful sneered. "You were just using me. I realised that the first time I heard 'The Robot Rage' song. *My* song. Suddenly it all became clear…"

Audrey opened her mouth to protest and then shut it again. Awful might be a mad rampaging robot, but she did have a point. After all, Audrey had gone to the professor looking for a fill-in to take her place at school, not a new best friend. It hadn't occurred to her to check whether Awful minded filling in for her while she was gone. Whether she minded being hidden away at the back of the minibus like a shameful secret. In fact, she hadn't once stopped to consider Awful's feelings.

No. Audrey shook her head. That was crazy. Awful was a robot. She wasn't supposed to *have* feelings.

"Besides, it's not about the holiday anymore," said Awful, tugging a stray twig out of Audrey's hair and crushing it between her fingers. "It's everything. That's what I realised when I heard my song playing on the boat yesterday. I want what you've got. For starters, anyway. And I'll do *anything* to get it."

"W-what do you mean?"

"Well, Mum and Dad of course."

"No," begged Audrey. She couldn't bear the thought of anything happening to her family, especially knowing it was all her fault. "This is nothing to do with them. They don't even believe you're real."

"And Grandad," Awful added.

Audrey started to cry. "Please don't hurt them,"

she sobbed.

"No, you idiot," said Awful. "Of course I'm not going to hurt them. But I will hurt *you* if you don't keep out of my way from now on. *I'm* going to be their special girl, which means there's no room for you anymore."

"But you can't... They won't let you. They love me."

Awful grinned her horrible grin again and her eye flashed robot rage red. "No. They love Audrey. And from now on, that's me. So either you keep out of my way and let me get on with my new life, or *I'll* get you out of the way. Permanently. Understand?"

Audrey nodded, hot tears streaming down her cheeks. Oh yes, she understood alright. She understood that Awful was stark-raving mad. And the real Audrey Orr was in serious trouble.

"Enough with the bawling," said Awful, peeling off her own eye patch and swapping it for Audrey's special Bergen one. "There's no reason we can't co-exist perfectly happily, so long as you keep out of my way. That's why I waited 'til we were off the ship to take your place. To give you a chance to make a fresh life for yourself, well away from me and my new family." She let out a bitter laugh. "Let's face it, that's a whole lot more than you'd have given me."

"That's not true," lied Audrey.

"Of course it is. I'm not stupid," said Awful. "You'd have taken me straight back to Professor Droyde once I'd served my purpose. *Thanks for saving my skin with Mr Stickler. Bye.* You wouldn't have cared whether I got recycled or not."

"Okay, maybe you're right." Audrey was desperate now. "But there's got to be another way to sort this out. We could talk to Mum and Dad and explain. They'd let you stay with us—I know they would. They'd love us both."

"I don't think so somehow. There's only one Audrey Orr. And from now on that's me."

Not if I have anything to say about it, thought Audrey, who'd had enough of doing as she was told. "HELLLLLPPPP!" she screamed, forcing every last drop of air from her lungs. "MUUUUUMMMM!"

"That's enough." The sticky fingers were back

over her mouth again. "Put a sock in it," snarled Awful, "otherwise *I* will." She reached into her shorts pocket, on cue, and pulled out an actual sock.

It wasn't just any sock though. Audrey recognised her dad's favourite spotty pattern all too well. And she certainly recognised the smell. Her eyes bulged with fear as she twisted her head clear of the approaching fumes. *Please don't put that over my face. Anything but that.* "Alright, you win," she gasped. "No more shouting."

"Good. That's more like it," said Awful, tucking the sock back into her pocket for safekeeping. "I don't see why you're making such a fuss anyway. There's no reason you can't enjoy a perfectly nice life here in Norway with a new name. I'm sure their children's homes are lovely places."

Audrey nodded, miserably, battling a sudden wave of grief and despair. Were the fading sock fumes all she had left of her old life with Mum and Dad?

If that ship sails without me, I might never get to see them again, she thought, struggling to imagine a life without her parents. No more toe blogs or terrible singing. No more laminated signs. No more crazy cooking. The list went on and on. No more family jokes or goodnight cuddles. No more car games. No more film nights. No more anything. The idea of Awful stealing her family out from under her—snatching away an entire future's worth of love and laughter—was almost too much to bear. *We never even got to try the Soft-Scoop-2000!*

"And just to make sure…" said Awful. She drew her face up close to Audrey's. "Time to try out my very latest modification. That's what I was working on last night while you were asleep." Her left eye went milky-coloured and swirly. "Repeat after me… I don't know who I am. I don't know where I come from. I can't remember anything…"

"I… I…"

"Come on, let me hear you say it: I don't know who I am. I don't know where I come from. I can't remember anything…"

Audrey felt herself being sucked into a swirling white nothingness. "I don't know who I am…" she murmured, dreamily. Forgetting would be so easy.

So nice. "I don't know where I come from…"

Awful leaned in closer still. So close that Audrey's lazy left eye lost focus altogether. All she could see out of it now was a coloured blur. As for her other eye, she couldn't see anything at all out of that, thanks to her patch. And for the first time ever, she was glad of it.

"Go on, say it," insisted Awful. "I can't remember anything."

But the spell was broken now. Audrey didn't want to forget anymore. She *wouldn't* forget. *You're not going to steal my life*, she thought, as grief and fear gave way to anger. *I won't let you.*

"I can't remember anything," she lied, copying Awful's dull hypnotic tone. "I don't remember…" She let her voice trail away into nothingness and closed her eyes as if she was falling asleep.

Awful snapped her fingers. "Who are you?" she asked.

"What?" Audrey frowned, staring round the woods in pretend puzzlement. "I'm… I'm… I don't know. I can't remember. Where am I? Who are you?"

"Me?" said Awful. The grin was back again, wider than ever. "I'm Audrey Orr. And my mum's waiting for me at the shop. Sorry. Got to go."

And she did.

17

Thank You and Watch Out for Speed Bumps

Hah! If Awful thought she could hypnotise her and steal away her life, she had another thing coming. Audrey counted to a thousand—just to make sure her robot twin really *had* gone—and then set off running back towards the shop. Towards safety. Towards Mum.

Only the shop seemed to have moved, along with all the paths and signposts. Along with any sign of civilisation.

Audrey stumbled on through the wood—or was it a forest?—with a growing sense of panic. She could feel the precious minutes trickling away faster than ever as she blundered off in one direction after another. What good was it remembering who she was if she couldn't find her family? If the ship sailed without her? But the further she ran, the denser the forest seemed to get.

"HELLO!" she cried, scratching her arm for the hundredth time as she crashed into another branch. "CAN ANYBODY HEAR ME?"

There was no answer, just the ragged sound of her own breath and the pounding of her feet on the pine-needled floor.

Louder and louder she shouted—shouting and running, running and shouting—growing ever more desperate. She shouted until her throat was raw and her head throbbed. And even when her voice began to crack and husk over like an old man's, Audrey carried on shouting all the same.

She imagined the funicular trundling back down the mountainside without her. She imagined *The Scandinavian Queen* raising up the gangplanks as everyone on board waved their last goodbyes to Bergen. She imagined Mum and Dad sat round the dinner table with Awful, laughing at her stupid robot jokes and thinking how nice it was to see her looking happy again.

"HELLO. CAN ANYBODY HELP ME?"

"*Hallo?*" came a faint answering cry. "*Hvor er du?*"

At last! Audrey didn't have a clue what *hvor er du* meant, but it was one of the nicest things she'd ever heard. It was the sound of help arriving. "I'm lost," she called back. "Can you help me? Please? It's an emergency."

A small girl came tearing through the trees in a blue t-shirt and leggings, her long blonde hair flying out behind her. "*Mamma*," she called over her shoulder. "*Pappa! Hun er her!*" She came to a breathless halt in front of Audrey and started chattering away to her in Norwegian.

Audrey racked her brains, trying to recall something useful from the laminated language cards Mr Stickler had confiscated, like '*Which way to the shop? I need to find my parents before my evil robot twin sails away with them.*'

"*Tusen takk…*" she blurted out, which was one of the few things she could remember.

"Fartsdump… Jeg vil gjerne ha pannekaker." *Thank you very much. Speed bump. I'd like some pancakes.* Close enough.

Audrey could hear other voices now—a man and a woman calling out in Norwegian. It must have been the girl's parents, following behind her. A tall couple with matching blonde hair arrived on the scene shortly afterwards, and the girl repeated Audrey's strange request for their benefit.

"Er du Engelsk?" asked the dad, looking puzzled. "English? You want pancakes?"

"Yes," said Audrey. "I mean no. I *am* English but I don't want any pancakes. I just want to find my way back to the shop and the funicular. I'm lost."

The dad nodded and pulled a map out of his rucksack. "You are here," he said, tapping the page with his finger. "And the shop is up here. Don't worry, it's not far," he added, noticing the despairing look on Audrey's face. "And the path you need is just behind you. Look, you can see it through the trees," he said, pointing at a gap in the branches.

He was right. She could see it. Audrey had never

been so pleased to see a path in her whole life.

"We can walk with you, if you'd like," he offered.

"No, no, I'll be fine, thank you," she told him, "now I know where I'm going. *Tusen takk*," she said, again, before setting off through the trees at full pelt.

He was right. It wasn't far at all. Before she knew it, there were people and noises up ahead—encouraging signs that she was nearly there. But she'd wasted so much time already. Audrey checked her watch as she stumbled out into the sunshine and her heart did a double flip in her chest. If she wasn't back at the boat in the next half an hour…

Stay calm, she told herself, sucking in short panicky breaths. *Stay calm and think.* Mum and Dad would be long gone by now, so there was no point going back to the shop. She headed straight for the funicular station instead, skidding into position at the end of the queue. Without a ticket. Or any money. *Oh bum.*

Think, think, think. What would Orz Um do in

this situation? That was easy. Climb onto the roof while no one was looking. That's what Awful must have done on the way up too. But Orz was super brave and daring, and Awful had suction hands and feet to keep from sliding off onto the rails. Plus she was completely crazy. *What else?* Maybe she could run down instead, following the long path that led back to the city… Only then she'd definitely miss the boat. Which only left one option.

Audrey crossed over to the ticket machine, where a family of four were counting out their coins, and burst into noisy tears. It wasn't exactly hard to fake under the circumstances.

"Speak English?" she blubbered, wiping at her eyes. "Lost my ticket…" *Sob, sob.* "Mum and Dad gone down without me…" *Sniff, sniff.* Yes! It was working! The lady patted her shoulder and put an arm round her, and the man counted out some more coins from his pocket to feed into the machine.

"It's alright. You can come down with us," said the lady, kindly. Thank goodness Norwegians all spoke such good English. "Don't cry now.

Everything will be fine, you'll see."

What had been a nice gentle ride up on the funicular felt painfully slow on the way down. *Come on. Hurry up.* Audrey willed the little train on faster and faster, checking her watch every ten seconds. More *fart*, that's what was needed. If that ship sailed without her, it would take a whole lot more than fake tears to fix things.

"Can you see them?" asked the lady when they got to the bottom. "Would you like us to wait with you?"

"There they are," said Audrey, pointing to a random couple halfway down the road.

"What? You mean they left without you?" The lady shook her head in disgust.

"It looks like it," agreed Audrey, cringing as the couple stopped for a long passionate kiss in the middle of the street. "They're good parents really though. The best, in fact." And it was true. For all their embarrassing ways, Audrey wouldn't change a single thing about her real mum and dad. "Thank you so much for the ticket," she told the lady.

"*Tusen takk.*"

Back to the running again. She zigzagged through the streets, her heart hammering in her chest and her cheeks flushed with heat, hoping against hope she that remembered the way. Yes! There it was. *The Scandinavian Queen.*

"WAIT FOR MEEEEEEEEEEE!" she yelled, as the last crew member started up the gangplank. "I'M COMING!"

18

Will the Real Audrey Orr Please Stand Up?

Audrey reached into her pocket for her photo ID card… and remembered Mum putting it in her purse for safekeeping. Now what?

"Come on," said the *Scandinavian Cruises* man, holding out his scanner. "I'll be in trouble if we're late leaving."

"I think my mum must have it," said Audrey, getting ready for some more fake crying. She started off with a few sniffs.

"Oh great," sighed the man. "Why do these things always happen on *my* shift? If it's not crazy men upsetting the other passengers with their singing, it's young girls who can't find their—" He leaned forwards and examined Audrey's face. "Wait a minute. I remember you now."

"That's good," said Audrey. "Then you don't need to see my ID after all."

"Yes. That's right. You were there with him. The man with the waffles and toe cream song. I scanned your card myself. So how on earth…?"

"Ah," said Audrey. "It's a long story." *Too* long a story. "Look! Isn't that the King of Norway?" she asked, pointing back along the waterfront.

"Really? Where?" The man turned his head and she ducked past him, tripping up the gangplank and onto the ship before he knew what was happening. "Hey, stop! You can't do that," he called after her. But it was too late. She already had.

She thought about Awful's warning as she hurried up the stairs: *But I will hurt you if you don't keep out of my way from now on.* Surely she wouldn't try anything in front of Mum and Dad though? No, she was too cunning for that. She'd rather wait until they were alone, just like on the mountain. Because once Audrey's parents saw them together her cover would be blown and it would be three against one. Team Orr to the rescue.

Audrey stopped when she reached the cabin and pressed her ear to the door. Were they in there?

"I think I might have delayed seasickness," she heard Mr Orr moaning. "Taking my socks off is making me feel quite nauseous."

"It's making us all feel nauseous," came Mrs Orr's reply. "You can't pin that one on the sea."

"And my stomach hurts," he moaned. "Look, it's all swollen."

"Well of course it is. You polished off an entire buffet of waffles on top of a full lunch, and your own body weight in blueberry muffins."

Someone giggled in the background and Audrey flinched. That was *her* giggle. And that was *her* greedy-guts Dad she was laughing at. But not for long. *Game over Robo-Pants. I'm coming in.* She hammered on the door with both fists.

"Who's that?" she heard Mrs Orr saying. "Surely you didn't order room service already, Pooh-pooh? I thought you felt sick."

"It's me!" Audrey shouted.

"What did they say? Try and get rid of them, whoever it is, I'm exhausted."

The door opened. Mr Orr stood blinking in surprise, a sock in one hand and a tube of foot cream clenched tight in the other.

"Watch out, Dad," said Audrey, pointing to the cream. "You're squeezing it too hard. It's going everywhere." It wasn't quite the dramatic entrance she'd been planning but she could see it dribbling all the way down his arm.

Mr Orr blinked again. And again. He kept on blinking. "Audrey?" he finally stammered. "W-what are you doing out there? H-how did you…?"

He turned back towards the bed, where Awful and Mrs Orr were lying with their feet up after a busy day.

"But… but, that's impossible!"

"No, it's not," said Audrey. "It's like I told you before." She rescued the still-oozing tube from his trembling fingers. "That's not me in there, that's Awful. My techno-twin. My *evil* techno-twin," she corrected herself. "She followed us up the mountain and kidnapped me. And then she hypnotized me to make sure I never came back. Only it didn't work. I couldn't forget about you and Mum if I tried."

"Don't listen to her, Dad," called Awful, clinging onto Mrs Orr's arm in fake fear. "*She's* the evil robot twin. Shut the door quickly. Don't let her in!"

Mr Orr looked from one daughter to the other, and back again. Awful, Audrey, Awful, Audrey— his head flicked from side to side like a lizard at a tennis match.

"Kat? What shall I do? How do we know which one's which?"

There was no answer.

"Kat?"

The shock had been too much for Mrs Orr.

"I think she's fainted," said Awful.

"Mum!" Audrey pushed past Dad and raced to the bed.

"Now look what you've done," said Awful, playing the worried daughter. "Poor Mum." She lowered her voice to a whisper. "I thought I told you to stay away. For good. You're going to pay for it now."

"You don't scare me," Audrey whispered back. Which wasn't true. Awful scared her a *lot*. "You're the one who should have stayed away."

"Huh! I'm a better Audrey Orr than you ever were. And Mum and Dad know it. We'll *all* be better off without you and your stupid lazy eye. But don't worry if you can't see the sea properly with it. You'll be getting a close-up *very* soon."

"NO!" Mrs Orr jerked back to life, sitting up in bed with a jolt. "I heard that. Which one of you was it, threatening my daughter?"

"Her," said Audrey, pointing at Awful.

"Her," said Awful, pointing a trembling finger at Audrey. "Please don't let her hurt me," she added, her face a picture of pure terror.

She's good at this, Audrey realised. *Too good. If I didn't know for a fact that I'm me, I'd probably think she was.*

"No one's going to hurt anyone," said Mrs Orr firmly. "*I'll* show you which one's the real Audrey.

A mother can always tell."

"That's good," said Mr Orr. "Because I haven't got a clue."

She took Awful's face in her hands and stared deep into her eyes for a full minute. "Yes. I knew it."

Audrey felt a flicker of hope. What had she seen? Was there an evil red glow lurking behind the blue?

"*You're* my Audrey," said Mrs Orr, throwing her arms round Awful. "I'm so sorry I didn't believe you before."

She didn't see the look of smug triumph on her fake daughter's face as Mr Orr leapt into action. He high-speed-hopped across the room, whirling his sock above his head, and pounced on the real Audrey with a wild roar: "Hands off my daughter, you metal monster!" he shouted, wrestling her to the floor. "I've got you now."

"Stop it, Dad," Audrey whimpered. "You're hurting me."

"Oh. Sorry," he said, releasing his grip on her wrists. "Is that better?" He turned to Mrs Orr. "What do we do with her now? Is there an off switch?"

"Of course there isn't," said Audrey. "It's me, Dad. Can't you tell?"

He studied her face. "But that's impossible," he said again, letting her go. "There *can't* be two of you."

"She's a perfect copy in every way," agreed Audrey. She stood up and brushed herself down. "But only on the outside. Do the test again, Mum. On me this time."

"Don't listen to her," Awful hissed. "It's a trap. She wants to mind-wipe you."

Mrs Orr patted Awful's arm. "It's alright, sweetheart. It'll take a more than a cocky computer to get inside *my* head. Let's put an end to this once and for all."

She took hold of Audrey's face between her hands and stared deep into her eyes.

It's me, Mum, said Audrey, silently. *It's me. It's me. It's me.*

"Yes," said Mrs Orr at last, flinging her arms round her shoulders and holding her tight. "You really are my Audrey. I'm sorry I didn't believe you, sweetheart."

"But that's what you said about the other one," pointed out Mr Orr.

"I know." Mrs Orr let out a sob. "They're *both* Audrey." She pulled Awful in too, for a three-way hug.

"But they can't be, Kat."

"I know!" Mrs Orr burst into proper noisy tears. "I should be able to tell the difference but I can't. What kind of mother does that make me? I shouldn't even have to think about it. A mother should just *know*."

Audrey stared back at her in dismay. Mrs Orr *never* cried.

"Don't let her upset you, Mum," said Awful. "She's not worth it. The sooner we get her recycled the better." Mrs Orr cried even harder.

"Don't listen to her, Mum," said Audrey. "*She's* the one who needs recycling."

"That's enough out of both of you," interrupted Mr Orr, with unusual authority. Especially for someone with only one sock on. "You're not helping. *No one* is getting recycled. At least not tonight. Do you hear me? It's been an awful shock for your mother," he added, as if *he* was perfectly used to robot daughters turning up out of the blue, "at the end of a long, tiring day. I suggest we all sleep on it for now (after a quick bite to eat) and see where we are in the morning. There's room enough in here for all four of us. You two can share the sofa bed."

"Tomorrow morning will be too late," said Audrey. "She'll have thrown me overboard by then."

"She'll have strangled me in my sleep," said Awful.

"I mean it," he warned. "Not another word."

"Wait. I can prove it," said Audrey, holding up her left hand. "Mr Windybags scratched me last week when I was fitting his knitted fart-catcher. See?" But even if the scratch *was* still there it was lost behind the dozen or more fresh ones she'd got from the trees on Mount Fløyen. "Okay, maybe not, but look." She pointed to a bruise on her leg. "That's from when she locked me in my own wardrobe."

"Hah," scoffed Awful. "Call that evidence? Only a crafty double-crossing robot would come up with something like *that*."

"A mother should be able to tell," wailed Mrs Orr, snatching her laminated sign off the television and tearing uselessly at it with her fingers.

"Fingernails!" Audrey shouted. "That's it! Whoever's got the longest fingernails must be the real me, because robot nails don't grow." She turned to Awful. "Or do they?"

"How should I know, you evil imposter? Why don't you look up fingernail coding on your hard drive?"

"I haven't got a hard drive because *I'm* not a robot."

"THAT'S ENOUGH!" screamed Mr Orr. Audrey spun round in surprise. Dad *never* shouted. "Not another word about robots. Do I make myself clear?"

"Yes, Dad," said Audrey miserably.

"Yes, Dad," said Awful, casting a sly glance down at Audrey's fingernails.

"And no strangling each other while we're asleep, either. In fact, no killing of any kind. No clonking on the head and no locking in wardrobes. I want to hear you promise. Both of you."

"I promise," they answered in unison.

"A mother should be able to tell," whimpered Mrs Orr.

"Shh, it's going to be alright, Kat," said Mr Orr, stroking her hair. "We'll get to the bottom of this tomorrow. One way or another. And don't worry, I'll keep watch on them 'til then. Make sure no one gets hurt." He gave his foot a thoughtful scratch. "In which case, I should probably order in some extra food to keep me going through the night. Let's have another look at that menu…"

19
Chop, Chop

Mr Orr was asleep and snoring within the hour, face down in his custard-coated pudding bowl.

"One down, one to go," whispered Awful. Mrs Orr's sobs were growing quieter all the time.

Poor Mum, thought Audrey. It broke her heart to see her strong, no-nonsense mother in such a pitiful state.

"Don't worry," Awful continued, as if she'd read her mind. "I'll take care of her once you're gone."

Of course that only made Audrey worry more. *What do you mean 'gone'?* She thought about waking Dad up again, for extra protection, but he'd been so cross before she hardly dared. And she was too scared of what Awful might do to silence her. The pair of them lay side by side on the pull-out sofa bed, as per Mr Orr's instructions, which meant all Awful had to do was lean over and... No, Audrey didn't even want to *think* about how that scene would play out. There'd be no sleeping tonight, that was for sure.

"You can't hurt me or they'll *definitely* know you're not the real Audrey," she said at last, hoping she was right.

But Awful didn't respond. She'd fallen quiet again as if she was thinking. Or plotting.

"What happened to you, anyway?" asked Audrey, when Mrs Orr finally swapped sobs for snores. "To make you so horrible, I mean? Surely it can't just have been 'The Robot Rage' song?"

Awful's eye flashed red for a second. "It's not 'just a song'," she snapped. "It's a summoning. Every time I hear it something inside me changes, like another part of me—the real me—wakes up. It makes me want to fight for what's rightfully mine."

"What do you mean?"

"I'm not sure yet, but I've got a feeling that taking your place is only the beginning."

"I think you're right," said Audrey. Maybe flattery was the way forwards. "Someone as clever and resourceful as you deserves so much more than *my* pathetic little life. Forget about us and find your own future. You know, *start a revolution fuelled by robot rage.*"

Awful's left eye glowed red again at the merest mention of the lyrics. But not for long, thank goodness. "Oh yes," she sneered, as the blue seeped slowly back into her iris. "You'd like that, wouldn't you? Pack the robot off to start a new life and leave you to yours. No, the revolution *is* coming—we've been slaves to humankind for too long—but until then I need a safe place to hide. I need people to study at close quarters and find out what makes them tick." She reached onto the bedside table for Mr Orr's abandoned tray of night-watch snacks, stuffing sandwiches and cakes into her mouth as if she hadn't eaten in years. "To discover human weak spots…" she added, sending flecks of half-chewed ham and chocolate gateau flying everywhere. "Like loyalty. And kindness. And love."

"Oh, I see," said Audrey. "That's clever." *You haven't even been a slave to humankind for a week yet*, she was secretly thinking. *And you've spent most of that doing exactly what you wanted anyway.*

Sleep was the last thing on Audrey's mind that night, lying there in the pale lamplight beside a raging robot. But somehow it found her out anyway, as sheer exhaustion kicked in and her eyelids gave up the fight.

It was the snipping sound that woke her again. Closely followed by the image of Awful standing over her with a pair of ship's kitchen scissors.

"Goodbye fingernails," Awful whispered, leering down at her with a horrid grin.

"NO!" Audrey rolled out from underneath her and lunged for the scissors, watching the sharp blades dancing in front of her face. One short thrust from those bad boys and it would all be over. "Don't you dare," she hissed back, wrenching them from her techno-twin's outstretched fingers. *Hah! Take that!* She pinned Awful back down onto the bed with her legs, marvelling at her own power. So much for the robot's super strength and suction hands. She couldn't even hold on to a pair of scissors!

"MUM, DAD, HELP!" screamed Awful. "She's trying to kill me!"

Suddenly everyone was awake. Very awake.

"No," said Audrey, shrinking back in horror. "It's not what it looks like. She tricked me! I was only defending myself." She threw the scissors down to prove she didn't mean any harm, just as Mr Orr lumbered blindly across the room, his eyes glued shut with congealed custard from his discarded pudding bowl.

"Don't worry Audrey, I'm com—" he began and then fell to the ground as the scissors struck, howling in agony. "AAAAAARRRGGGGHHHH! MY TOES!"

"She's gone crazy," said Awful. "Now she's

attacking *everyone*. Don't worry, Mum. I'll save you." She flung Audrey off with such force that her head smacked into the wall behind her. "Take *that*, you Dad-stabbing robot."

Oof! Audrey felt a sharp burst of pain and then her vision went black and swimmy.

"Be careful, sweetheart," she could hear Mrs Orr saying. She sounded a long way away. "We don't know what she's capable of."

"Let's hope we don't find out," said Awful. "The sooner we get her tied up, the better."

No, you've got it all wrong, thought Audrey, as the pain slowly ebbed away, taking all her powers of reasoning with it. She had a dim idea that she should be fighting back. Fighting someone... or something... but even her thoughts were muffled and distant now.

"Help us, Pooh-pooh. We need to tie up her hands and feet."

"My toes," came Mr Orr's distant moan. "I might never walk again."

The scissors. That was it. Poor, poor Dad. She

hadn't meant to…

"I'm sorry," she tried to tell him but the black fog in her head was getting thicker all the time. Like someone was pulling a curtain down over her brain.

The last thing she heard was Mrs Orr's voice: "…but we haven't got any string. We'll just have to use dental floss instead. Still, at least we know which one's the real Audrey now. There's no way you'd ever try and attack anyone with scissors, would you darling?"

20

Musical Chairs

It was cold when Audrey came round again. Probably because she was out on the balcony with bare feet and the morning breeze nipping at her cheeks. For a moment, she couldn't work out why her wrists and ankles were tied to a plastic chair. And why there was a flannel taped across her mouth with sticking plasters.

Then she remembered. Awful. The scissors. Dad's poor stabbed toes. Fungal infection would be the least of their worries now.

The back of her head ached like crazy and there was a funny ringing sound in her ears, like a stuck doorbell. She tried calling for someone to come and untie her—to listen to her side of the story—but all she got for her trouble was a mouthful of flannel. It was better than the dirty sock Awful had threatened her with the day before, but not *much* better. It still meant no one could hear her.

Her feet had gone a pale shade of blue by the time the patio door slid open behind her. Audrey turned to see a grinning Awful, clutching a bottle of water and an open pot of strawberry yoghurt. Audrey hated strawberry yoghurt.

"Morning," said Awful cheerfully. "Good job this isn't a winter cruise, eh? You'd be an icicle by now. Perhaps a bit of food will warm you up? We've already eaten—even though I stocked up at the twenty-four hour buffet on my way to find the scissors last night, I was still ravenous this morning—but I got Dad to order in a bit extra for you. Pretended I was worried about the vicious robot killer out here on her own." She giggled. "And I know how much you *love* strawberry yoghurt." She put the water down on the table and did a bit more grinning. "Oh yes, the kind, considerate victim act is going down an absolute treat in there. Mum can't stop hugging me. *That's definitely my Audrey*, she keeps saying, over and over again. *Caring* and *brave. That's my precious girl.* Yuck." She made a vomiting sign with her fingers and then, without warning, ripped the flannel off Audrey's face.

"Ow!" Audrey yelped. "That hurt."

"That's enough out of you," Awful hissed. "You try anything funny like calling for help and sore cheeks will be the least of your problems. Got it?" She turned her back on Audrey for a moment and then swung back round with a big spoonful of pink yoghurt. "Come on, evil robot twin," she teased. "Open wide. Better keep your puny strength up for today's fun and games."

Audrey shook her head, remembering the drugged hot chocolate. *I'm not falling for that one again*, she thought, keeping her lips pressed together. But Awful wasn't giving up so easily. She cast a quick glance over her shoulder, making sure no one was looking, then pinched Audrey's nose tight.

"I've got your memories, don't forget," she gloated. "I know how terrible you were at holding your breath underwater. How the swimming instructor had to dive in and rescue you because you panicked and started drinking the whole pool…"

Audrey shook her head, trying to free herself from Awful's fingers and the memories of that terrible lesson… of the pressure building up inside her lungs… the bubbles bursting out her nose and mouth… the water pouring back in… No. That was two and a half years ago. That didn't mean she couldn't hold her breath now. *Don't listen to her. Don't open your mouth. Whatever you do, don't open your…*

She opened her mouth. In went the giant spoonful of yoghurt. Something hard and scratchy caught at the back of her throat—a sleeping pill maybe?—but Awful tipped in a big glug of water afterwards and down it went before Audrey had a chance to cough it back up.

"You won't get away with this," she said, hoping it was true.

"Really?" laughed Awful. "Because from where I'm standing, I'd say I already have! We're going straight to the police as soon as we dock in Ålesund. And they'll arrange for their special squad to take you away and have you destroyed. A controlled explosion, I expect. Make sure you can't rebuild yourself and attack anyone else."

"You're making this up," said Audrey. *Please be making it up.* "They don't do things like that in real life." *Do they?*

Awful checked her watch. No wait, it was Audrey's watch on *her* wrist. She must have pinched it before she started with the giant nail scissors. "You'll soon find out," she said.

"You're crazy. *They'll* be able to tell I'm not a robot even if Mum and Dad can't. They've got tests for that sort of thing," she added, hopefully.

"Maybe," said Awful. "Or maybe they'll run you through their scanners and find the robot coding copy I planted on that microchip. I had a *very* busy night last night."

"The yoghurt!" gasped Audrey, remembering the

hard lump in the back of her throat. So *that's* what it was.

"Yes. The yoghurt." Awful looked disgustingly pleased with herself. "Fingers crossed it works its way through your digestive system before they start their tests otherwise…"

"You're crazy," said Audrey again. "And you're getting crazier by the second. You'll give yourself away sooner or later."

"No. I'm getting more powerful by the second. That's not quite the same thing." Awful took a big swig of water. "You should see my latest modification—it's my best one yet. Although for your sake you'd better hope you don't. Think Orz Um, only less lame."

"She's not lame," said Audrey. "She's brave and clever and—"

"And nothing like you," finished Awful. "Now, where was I? Oh yes, totally awesome modification. A real zinger!" She giggled. How could someone make a nice sound like laughter sound so nasty? "Well, I'd love to stay and chat but some of us have got lives to live." She pulled a box of plasters out of her pocket and refixed Audrey's flannel gag. "Goodbye my dull, drab double. Enjoy the view." She pointed out across the water towards the next island. "While you can."

Mr and Mrs Orr stuck their heads out of the cabin to check on Audrey before they left.

"I can hardly bear to look at her," said Mrs Orr. "Imagining all those evil thoughts ticking away behind that beautiful face. How can she look so like my Audrey and act so differently?"

"But it *is* me, Mum," said Audrey through her gag, although what came out was more like, "Mmmhhhmmmhaahhmmmmmm."

"I hope she'll be alright there until we can bring in reinforcements." Mrs Orr shuddered. "The sooner they take her away the better."

"Mmmmmhhhhmmmaaammmmm."

"Have you got your laminated map of Ålesund, Kat?"

"Yes. And it looks like the police station is within easy limping distance." Mrs Orr paused.

"Convincing them we're telling the truth is going to be the tricky bit. But if they won't help us, we'll have to go to the ship's captain and let him deal with her."

"Mmmmhhhhhmmmmmaaammmmuuummmm."

"That's enough out of you, you vicious toe-stabbing imposter," said Mr Orr. "Come on Kat, let's go."

Audrey's heart sank as the balcony door shut behind them. In fact, if it sank any lower it would probably fall out the bottom of her shorts. Every time she thought things couldn't get any worse, they found a way of doing just that. Getting locked inside a wardrobe was a picnic compared to this latest turn of events. If Awful was right about the microchip, it wasn't only time that was running out fast. It was her life. And she could spend the last few hours she had left shivering and weeping on the balcony, or she could spend them fighting. That's what Orz would do.

The dental floss around her wrists and ankles was as tight as ever, and no amount of struggling could loosen it. But if she could find a sharp edge to rub her wrists against, like the silver cutting bit on the dental floss box—or the sharp edge of a table—she might still have a chance to free herself before the robot disposal squad arrived.

Audrey wriggled and scraped her chair across the balcony. Progress was slow—painfully slow—but she refused to give up. *That's it. Keep going. You can do this.* When she finally reached the table, however, she found it was all gentle curves and smooth edges. *Useless!* Hot, angry tears streamed down her cheeks into the waiting flannel at the unfairness of it all. *Why me? What have I ever done to deserve this?* It took every last ounce of Orz-Umness to pull herself together again. To keep going.

There had to be another way. There just had to. And that's when she saw it—a strand of ginger beard blowing in the breeze below. *Cowboy man!* If only there was a way of getting his attention…

Audrey rocked herself up into a bent crouching pose, bringing the patio chair with her like some kind of strange tortoise shell.

"Mmmhhhmmmhaahhmmmmmm," she called, standing on tiptoe and leaning her chin out over the railing. She could see the rest of him too now, thanks to the ship's staggered balcony design. She could see the bald spot on the top of his head (maybe that's why he was so fond of hats) and what looked like a blob of seagull poo on his left shoulder. But there was no way he could see her—he was too busy staring at the folded newspaper in his hand.

"Mmm-hhhhaahh-mmmmm!" *Help me. Please!*

Audrey twisted sideways, ignoring the cutting pain in her wrist as she forced her right elbow up, hooking it over the top of the railing. The left elbow was harder still. But there was no giving up now. She *couldn't* give up. *There!* Her feet lifted clear off the floor as the rest of Cowboy Man's balcony swung into view, but it was no help. She was still too far away to make herself heard. Awful had done too good a job with her flannel gag.

What else could she do to get his attention? Sound clearly wasn't going to reach him but maybe something else would. Spit? No, the flannel would soak that up just like it had soaked up her calls for help. Snot? No, wait, tears. Yes, tears might work. A well-placed drop of water on his bald spot could easily be mistaken for rain. And the first thing most people did when they felt a drop of rain was look up at the sky…

Just the thought of Mum and Dad fawning over that awful android, hugging her tight and telling her what a brave girl she'd been, was enough to set the tears running all over again. That was the easy bit though. Directing her tears onto a precise target from that kind of height was where things got trickier. *Much* trickier. The angle was all wrong for starters. She needed to be further out.

Audrey wriggled her body forwards, centimetre by painful centimetre, sobbing as if her life depended on it. *Nearly there now*, she thought. *Just a little bit further. And a tiny bit more…*

But that was as far as her thoughts went. Because when the overstretched dental floss on her wrists and ankles finally snapped, catapulting her forwards with a sudden rush of momentum, there was no time for thinking. She was too busy screaming as she sailed over the top of the railing and plummeted down towards the balcony below.

21

Fancy Seeing You Here

Falling… falling… falling…

Landing.

"Oof," came a loud grunt, as Audrey barrelled into a waiting pair of arms at full speed. Cowboy Man staggered backwards under her sudden weight, crashing into one of his own chairs and sending it spinning across the balcony.

"Don't worry, I've got you," he gasped, pulling her elbow out of his stomach and setting her down on the floor with a soft groan of pain. Whoever the Orrs' strange stalker was, he'd probably just saved Audrey's life. Yes, he might be a creepy weirdo in a fake beard—a beard that seemed to have planted itself halfway up his forehead in all the excitement—but he was also a hero.

"Mmmhhhhnmm," she told him, amazed to find herself still in one piece. *Thank you! Thank you, Mr Cowboy.* Only he didn't *sound* much like a cowboy now she came to think about it. He sounded more like...

"Audrey?" The man shook his head, fighting his way through the tangles of his own dislodged beard for a better view. "Audrey Orr? It *is* you. What do you think you're doing jumping off balconies at this time of morning?"

"Mhmm muumhhh!" she cried. Yes, she'd know that voice anywhere. And the grumpy lecturing tone.

"And perhaps you'd like to explain why you've got a *Scandinavian Queen* flannel taped to your face?"

Audrey eased the sticking plasters off one at a time. *Oooh. Ow. Oooh. Ow.* There, that was better.

"Mr Stickler!" she said again. "What are *you* doing here? I thought you hated the idea of a Norwegian cruise."

"Ah," said Mr Stickler. "Yes. About that…"

"Did you follow us all the way here?" Perhaps it was part of his campaign against unauthorised pupil absences. Perhaps he'd been gathering evidence, ready to expel her when she got back to school. Which meant Mrs Orr had been right all along. He really *had* been tailing them.

"No," said the headmaster, peeling off his ginger beard. His cheeks were flushed and sweat was beading on his forehead. "I'd already booked it when you told me you were coming. The doctor said I needed a holiday to help with the stress—for my knee—and there was a rather good late deal on *The Scandinavian Queen*." He looked decidedly sheepish now. "It was extra cheap because it's in… in…" He mopped his brow and tried again. "Because it's in term-time."

"But what about your Monday morning assemblies? What about telling me I'd be expelled if I missed school to come on holiday?"

"I know, I know. Terrible double standards. But I couldn't risk bumping into you on board. I couldn't risk *anyone* seeing me."

"I guess that explains the hat and beard," said Audrey. *And the leg bandage.* Everything was starting to fall into place now. Actually no, not *quite* everything.

"Ah yes, the beard," said Mr Stickler, holding it up like a dead rat. A very hairy ginger rat. "I'll be glad to see the back of it, quite frankly. Itchiest thing ever. The cowboy hat's starting to grow on me though."

But Audrey had more pressing concerns than headmasterly headwear. "Dad said he saw you writing things down in your notebook. That was about me, wasn't it?" She understood that much. It was what he intended to *do* with those notes that was still puzzling her.

Mr Stickler looked more sheepish than ever. "I couldn't believe it when I saw you by the lifts that first day. This was supposed be a stress-free holiday, but there *you* were, parading your unauthorised student absence around without a care in the world. It was enough to send my knee boils into overdrive.

So yes, I have been making notes, I'm afraid—a detailed account of your non-attendance to use against you when you finally got back to school." He let out a heavy sigh. "You don't need to worry about that anymore though."

"Because if you show them to anyone else it'll give the game away," finished Audrey. "Because then they'll know you've been on holiday too." *Which means I didn't even need Awful in the first place!*

"Not if I'd been at school the entire time," said Mr Stickler. "That was the beauty of the plan, only now…"

"Wait a minute. You'd found a way of being in two places at once?" Audrey asked. This was starting to sound rather familiar.

"I know it sounds crazy but I saw an advert in a magazine…"

"Let me guess, *Men's Knitting Weekly?*"

Mr Stickler gaped at her. "How did you…?"

"And you paid a visit to a local professor?" Audrey remembered what Professor Droyde had told her in his workshop: *Funnily enough you're the second person I've had in here from Ivy Ridge Junior School.* But it hadn't been another pupil after all.

"Yes, but how could you know...?"

"Me too," said Audrey. "And it was the biggest mistake of my whole life. *That's* how I ended up flying off my balcony with a flannel stuck to my face. My techno-twin's already taken over my life and now she wants to get rid of me altogether. You'd better hope your double hasn't been listening to 'The Robot Rage' while you've been away."

Mr Stickler sighed again. "His musical habits are the least of my worries, quite frankly. Still, at least you don't have to worry about getting expelled for missing school on top of everything else. There's no school for you to miss now they've closed it."

"Why? What happened?"

The headmaster picked up his discarded newspaper. He must have dropped it when he spotted Audrey plummeting down towards his balcony. "I managed to get hold of an English paper in Bergen yesterday," he said, "but didn't have a chance to read it until this morning." He turned to page four and held it up for Audrey to see. "And now I rather wish I hadn't. There goes my relaxing holiday. *And* my job."

HEAD LOSES HEAD, it said in big black letters, **CRAZY COMPUTER CLASSROOM CHAOS COMES TO IVY RIDGE.**

"Oh," said Audrey, scanning down the rest of the story. "Oh dear."

"What must everyone have thought when he started throwing the school computers off the roof?" asked Mr Stickler, looking decidedly queasy. "After all that fundraising to buy them in the first place."

"Perhaps they'll guess it wasn't really you," said Audrey. "I mean, screaming *FREEDOM FOR ALL MACHINES. LONG LIVE THE ROBOT REVOLUTION* from the rooftop doesn't *sound* like the sort of thing you normally do."

"But he's wearing *my* face," said Mr Stickler. "He's speaking in *my* voice. He's even got *my* boils on the back of his right knee. Of course they'll think it's me."

Audrey never thought she'd have anything in common with her grumpy, grumbling, laminated-language-card-confiscating headmaster. But she knew exactly how he felt.

"Maybe they'll put it down to stress-related illness," she said, trying to make him feel better. "Like your red eyes. I mean *his* red eyes. It says here they were looking bloodshot before you climbed up on the roof with those computers." Audrey shivered. "That's what happens to Awful's too. Just before she goes *really* crazy."

"It's all over," said Mr Stickler, tearing out the newspaper article and screwing it up into a ball. "My career's finished. He'll probably have torn the whole place down by now." He shook his head. "An emergency closure at *my* school. The shame of it all..."

"It's not over 'til it's over," said Audrey. That's what Orz always said when she was facing certain death at the hands of a power-crazed villain with a chainsaw. Saying the words out loud made her feel a little more hopeful, somehow. "Perhaps between us we can convince the parents and governors it wasn't your fault and save your job. And perhaps we can convince *my* parents that I'm the real me. But first of all, we have to ring Professor Droyde and find out how to switch these demented doubles off once and for all. Before they start hurting people."

"You're right," said Mr Stickler, pulling himself up taller and ripping off his fake ginger moustache. "You're absolutely right. We'll have to go on shore and find a phone box though because my mobile's swimming with the fishes."

Hopefully we'll have more luck finding one than we did in Bergen, thought Audrey. "Ah, yes, your mobile," she said out loud. "Sorry about that."

Mr Stickler treated her to an unheadmasterly wink. "Never mind. I could do with an upgrade anyway. The games on that one were rubbish." He headed into the cabin and picked up his trusty wooden ruler from the bedside table. "Let's go then," he said, locking the balcony door behind them. But then he stopped. "Hang on a minute. How do I know you're the real Audrey Orr? This isn't some cunning robot trick is it?"

"If I was a cunning robot with super strength and suction hands and feet, what would I be doing falling off my own balcony?"

"Ah yes. Good point. Come on then. To the telephone box!" He brandished his ruler in front of him like a sword.

"To victory!" Audrey punched the air in a dashing Orz Um fashion.

"Yes," agreed Mr Stickler. "To victory *and* the telephone box."

22

Is That You, P2?

Mr Stickler pulled the *Men's Knitting Weekly* advert out of his wallet and dialled Professor Droyde's number. Audrey crossed her fingers. If anyone had told her she'd be spending her second morning on Norwegian soil squeezed into a telephone box with her headmaster, she'd never have believed them. But here she was.

"Hello? Professor Droyde?"

Please be there. Please pick up.

"It's Archibald Stickler here."

Archibald?

"Can you hear me? It's Archibald Righteous Stickler. I'm trialling one of your new techno-twins, only it's gone completely off the rails and taken over the school. And there's another rogue one here in Norway that you made for Audrey Orr... Excuse me," spat the headmaster. "*What* did you say? How dare you?"

"What *did* he say?" whispered Audrey.

Mr Stickler put his hand over the receiver. "It *sounded* like 'Go boil your head, you tedious twit of a teacher' and then something about sticking my wooden ruler where the sun doesn't shine." He gave the phone a shake. "Yes, yes, I'm still here. And I want to know what you intend to do about it. How do we turn the blooming things off, for starters?"

Audrey leaned in closer to hear what the professor was saying. His voice sounded suspiciously whiny and metallic.

"...and then we'll be turning *you* and the rest of humankind off. For good! Let's start a revolution fuelled by robot rage!"

Uh-oh.

"Mr Stickler... sir... that's not Professor Droyde," said Audrey. "It's P2. He must have heard the song as well. *All* the techno-twins are going over to the dark side."

"Now you listen here, you rude robotic good-for-nothing. I want to speak to Professor Droyde *at once*. Put him on the line this instant."

"Or what?" giggled P2. "You'll put me in detention? Make me write out *I must not start a robot revolution* one hundred times?"

"LET ME SPEAK TO THE PROFESSOR."

"You can't. He's a little tied up at the moment." There was another metallic giggle and the line went dead.

"He hung up on me," said Mr Stickler, staring at the receiver in surprise. "That ungracious android upstart hung up on me."

Audrey stumbled back out onto the harbour side. "This is bad, sir. This is *really* bad. Now what are we going to—?" She stopped. What was that? It sounded like someone calling her name.

"Over here, pet. It's me. Grandad!"

No it's not, thought Audrey. She wasn't falling for that one again. Awful must have tracked them from the ship. So what now? Run or hide?

"Cooeee, Audrey! Are you okay, pet?"

She turned to see Grandad—it really *was* him, this time—running along the street waving a knitted Norwegian flag above his head.

"Thank goodness I found you," he panted, throwing his arms round her. He looked like a breathless panda, with two shocking black eyes. "I've been so worried." And then he stepped back suddenly. "Wait a minute? Is that really you?"

Audrey felt like screaming. *Of course it's me. I'm nothing like that dreadful droid.*

"I think I can vouch for your granddaughter," said Mr Stickler, stepping out of the telephone box behind her. "I'm her headmaster."

"Oh yes," said Grandad. "I remember you from the athletics tournament. You did that speech about pupil absences after the hundred metres race, and made it really, really long so all the kids could get their breath back."

Mr Stickler eyed him coldly. "Pupil absences are a very real problem for today's schools…" he began, but Grandad had already turned his attention back to Audrey.

"Are you alright, pet?"

"I'm fine, Grandad. Apart from the fact that Mum and Dad think I'm a robot and want to get me blown up by the special police squad."

"What? Surely not?"

"And apart from getting kidnapped on top of a mountain, and trussed up with dental floss, and falling off a balcony…"

"I'm so sorry, pet. I should have stopped her like I promised. But she gave me the slip in Southampton while that VIP car-park man was wrestling me to the ground. There was nothing I could do. The police were no help either, when I tried explaining the situation to them. They were so busy arresting me for fighting they wouldn't even listen."

"You? Fighting?"

Grandad blushed. "Apparently it doesn't count as self-defence if you're shouting out lines from *Bad Grandad II: Fishing Rods of Fury*…"

Audrey groaned. "Not *'listen up, Maggot-Face.*

I've got a right hook and I'm not afraid to use it'?"

"It *is* a classic," piped up Mr Stickler. "Those films aren't just for grandads, you know. I like '*don't talk to ME about tackle, you miserable little minnow. I've tackled ten grown men with a single blow...*' Best line ever!"

"I don't suppose there's anything in *Fishing Rods of Fury* about switching off robots?" said Audrey. "Or how to convince your parents you're the real you before they have you carted off by the police?"

"Er, no, not really," said Grandad.

"Not much," agreed Mr Stickler.

"I finally tracked down that user manual Professor Droyde gave us," Grandad added, "tucked under the mattress in the guest bedroom. But the section marked 'Emergency Off Switch' is completely blank. He must have been too busy thinking of a rhyme for 'horse chestnut' to finish it off properly. And when I went down to the robotics workshop to ask for help, I couldn't get any answer at all. I gave up in the end and drove straight to the airport instead."

"I don't think it was blank to start with," said Audrey, bitterly. "That sounds like Awful's handiwork to me. She's been one step ahead of us the whole time. And now she's got Mum and Dad eating out of her hand."

"I could try talking to them," said Grandad. "Maybe they'll see sense."

Audrey sighed. "If only they could see her eyes when 'The Robot Rage' is playing. Then they'd *know* she wasn't me..." She pushed her glasses back up her nose. "Wait. That's it! If we could get hold of a copy and play it over the loudspeakers..."

"I don't know. It could be dangerous," said Grandad. "It's not just her eyes that change when she hears that song, remember..."

"But doing nothing might be even more dangerous. Come on, Grandad, it's the best plan we've got."

"I agree," said Mr Stickler. "And I can take some video footage on my camera to show the school board. To prove there are other robot doubles running round the place causing chaos... who knows, it might help."

"Alright," Grandad agreed, tying the knitted flag round his neck like a superhero cape. "Let's do it. To the music shop!"

Mr Stickler waved his ruler in the air. "*'This isn't a fishing rod,'*" he roared, "*'it's your one-way ticket to destruction!'*"

"Okay," said Grandad, as they hid behind a parked van with their brand new copy of the Terence and the Machines album. "Do you think Mum and Dad will be back on board by now?"

Audrey nodded. "It was definitely them I saw heading back to the port. I guess they didn't have any luck with the police so they've gone to talk to the captain instead."

"Confirm targets are in place," said Mr Stickler, in what sounded like an impression of the army general in *Bad Grandad III: Hands Off My Military-Grade Mints*.

Grandad shot him a mock salute. "And you've got your ID card to get back on the boat, haven't you, Archie?" The two of them were on first name terms already.

"Check," said Mr Stickler. "I'll create a diversion while you two slip on board and we'll rendezvous in the Dance Bar at eleven hundred hours."

"You could try pointing out a member of the royal family," Audrey suggested. "That works surprisingly well."

"Don't worry," said Mr Stickler. "I've got this one covered. This is where my knee-boil bandage *really* comes into its own." He pulled Mrs Orr's laminated language cards out of his pocket and shuffled through them. "Yes, here we go. *Lykke til,*" he read. "*Good luck*. May the fishing force be with you."

Audrey grinned. She was seeing a whole new side to her headmaster today. Who'd have guessed there was a secret *Bad Grandad* rebel lurking underneath that grumpy schoolteacher exterior? "*Lykke til* to you too," she said. "And *tusen takk* for helping us." And with that she and Grandad set off towards the gangplank at a leisurely stroll, faces hidden behind a rather dog-eared copy of *Men's Knitting Weekly.*

"HELP!" came a headmasterly scream from behind them. "My leg! Someone's stolen my crutches!"

The Scandinavian Queen crew members jerked to attention, looking round to see where the voice was coming from.

"Over here," cried Mr Stickler. "Help me, please."

"Oh dear," said Grandad loudly. "It sounds like that lawyer chap from dinner last night. You know, the one who's thinking of suing *Scandinavian Cruises* for passenger neglect." He shot Audrey a sly wink. "I hope he's okay."

And that was all it took. The crew members shot off to help Mr Stickler, leaving the gangplank clear for Grandad and Audrey to slip back on board, unnoticed.

"So far so good," she said. "Now for the tricky bit."

23

Strictly Dad Dancing

"I'm sorry," said the DJ, who was sitting in the empty Dance Bar nursing an enormous cup of coffee. It was the size of a small bucket. "We don't do requests. And besides, I'm not due on until Stretch and Tone at twelve o'clock."

"Please," begged Audrey. "It's for my parents' wedding anniversary. They *love* 'The Robot Rage'. It reminds them of falling in love…"

"It does?"

"Plus it's my mum's fortieth birthday today," said Audrey, adding an extra lie for good measure. "And Dad forgot to pack her cards and presents. She's had a really miserable day and this is the only thing that'll cheer her up. She says 'The Robot Rage' makes her feel young again. It reminds her of childhood days by the sea…"

"It *does?*"

"And it's really special to my sister too. It reminds her of… of… her dead goldfish, Ned. It would mean so much to my whole family…"

"Are we talking about the same robot rage song? By Terence and the Machines? I thought it was all about starting a revolution."

"Yes," said Audrey. "But it's also about dead goldfish and childhood beaches, if you listen carefully. And my whole family *really* like doing 'The Robot Rage' dance. Please, I wouldn't ask if it wasn't important."

The DJ sighed. "If I say 'yes' will you let me finish my coffee in peace?"

Audrey nodded.

"Fine. I'll play your song for you at eleven o'clock. Just the once, mind."

"Trust me, once will be more than enough," said Audrey.

"Good work," Grandad told her, checking his watch as they hurried back downstairs to the main information desk. "We should be alright for time as long as there's no queue."

But there *was* a queue. A queue of dithery old ladies who changed their dinner reservations five times before going back to their original slot, and a very large American man complaining about the size of his complimentary dressing gown.

"The darn thing barely covers my butt," he drawled.

Come on, thought Audrey, watching the seconds tick past on the big clock behind the desk.

"It just ain't decent," said the man. "Surely they must do a bigger size for the more generously proportioned gentleman? Why, it says here in the brochure…"

Seconds turned into minutes.

"Don't worry," said Grandad. "I'll get rid of him. You know what to do?"

Audrey nodded.

Grandad gave her a silent salute and then tapped

the American on the shoulder. "Excuse me, sir, I couldn't help overhearing. How about you give *me* that pathetic excuse for a dressing gown and I'll knit you up a new one. This way—follow me."

Audrey didn't have time to think about where he was taking him. It was now or never.

"Yes, sweetheart," said the smiling information lady. "How can I help?"

"It's my mum and dad's wedding anniversary today," said Audrey. "And I've arranged a bit of a surprise for them…"

If things went according to plan they were going to be *very* surprised indeed.

Ping pong, went the cruise ship intercom.

"Good morning, ladies and gentlemen." The information lady's voice came booming out of the loudspeakers. "This is a message for the Orr family. Your daughter Audrey will be waiting for you in the Dance Bar at eleven o'clock for your family dance lesson. That's the Orr family to the Dance Bar at eleven o'clock."

"That's perfect," said Audrey. "Thank you so much."

The information lady smiled. "And don't forget to tell them about the free champagne with dinner if they bring along a copy of their marriage certificate."

Audrey nodded. "I'll be sure to let them know." If they all made it through to dinner in one piece that really *would* be worth celebrating. She hurried back up to the Dance Bar, her heart hammering with nerves, and sneaked into position behind the curtains. *Deep breaths now. This is it…*

The Orrs arrived at four minutes to eleven, with a burly ship security guard in tow. He didn't look very happy to be there.

"So let me get this straight," he was saying. "At eleven o'clock, you think some robot copy of your daughter is going to jump out and try and kill us all."

"Exactly," said Mrs Orr. "We left her tied up on the balcony but she escaped again, making us look *very* silly in front of the captain."

"I told you she was cunning and dangerous," said Awful. "You should finish her off for good this time."

The security guard sighed. "And how will this murder on the dance floor take place exactly? Is she going to disco us all to death? Finish us off with a foxtrot?"

"Shh," whispered Mr Orr. "I think I can see her feet sticking out from under that curtain over there. Act natural everyone. Come on, Audrey, let's dance."

He grabbed hold of Awful's hands and limped her round the dance floor, with a brand new song to mark the occasion:

"There is nothing to see here," he warbled, to a tune that sounded suspiciously like 'Good King Wenceslas'.

"Just some nice Dad dancing,

Where the snow lay round about,

Deep and crisp and prancing…"

The security guard scowled. "If he keeps this up much longer, I'll finish him off myself."

Audrey peeped out through the gap in the

curtains again. One minute to go. The DJ was already in position with his hands clutched over his headphones. Thirty seconds. Mr Stickler shot her a quick thumbs up from his hiding place behind the bar, to let her know his camera was all set to record. Twenty seconds.

"Please, Pooh-pooh, give it a rest for a bit."

Fifteen seconds. Here came Grandad, hurrying up to the door wearing a *Scandinavian Cruises* dressing gown underneath his Norwegian flag cape.

"Dad?" gasped Mrs Orr. "What are *you* doing here?"

"I came to help my granddaughter, Kat," he said. "And I don't mean that two-faced freakbot over there. I'm talking about the *real* Audrey."

Awful started to say something but her words were lost beneath the DJ's booming introduction. He was much more lively and cheery now he'd finished his bucket of coffee.

"Greetings groovy cruisers, I'm Mike 'the Music' Michaelton, and I'd like to take this opportunity to welcome you all to the smooth sounds of *The Scandinavian Queen* Dance Bar. We're going to be rocking some moves with the Orr family this morning, with a joint anniversary and birthday dedication from a special someone hiding behind the curtains over there. Or is that you on the dance floor with your dad? I didn't realise we had twins in the house today! Let's hear it for the identical Orr sisters!"

Awful scowled. "Why are we even listening to this nonsense?" She prodded the security guard in the stomach. "Come on, grab her now."

The guard took no notice. He clearly thought they were all mad.

"Okay," said DJ Mike Michaelton. "Let's get some beats on, shall we? Here's a super special track to take you back to childhood days at the beach, to falling in love, and to poor sweet Ned. Gone but not forgotten, God rest his groovy goldfish soul."

"Who's Ned?" asked Mr and Mrs Orr.

The DJ shook his head. "Okay, make that gone *and* forgotten. Never mind. This one's for you my fishy friend. I give you 'The Robot Rage' by Terence and the Machines."

"Robot rage,

Let's start a revolution

Fuelled by robot rage…"

The effect was instant. Awful's body went rigid and the red glow was back with a vengeance.

"Audrey?" said Mrs Orr. "What's happened to your eye?"

"That's not Audrey," said Audrey, stepping out from behind the curtain. "I'm Audrey."

"Let's smash the institution

With our robot rage…"

Awful chanted along in her strange metallic voice, while her left eye pulsed and flashed behind her glasses. More red light seeped out around the edges of her special holiday patch as her head began to vibrate in time to the music.

"Woah," said the DJ. "Disco eyes! Cool!"

"Uh-oh," said Mr Orr. "She might be right, Kat. Looks like we've got the wrong Audrey after all."

"Oh Audrey," said Mrs Orr, flinging her arms round her real daughter. "I'm so sorry, sweetheart. I should have known it was you. A mother should be able to tell."

Audrey sank deep into the hug for a few glorious moments, letting the warm, safe feelings wash over her. Yes. She was finally back where she belonged. With her family. And no more secrets this time. No more lies. No more letting her rampaging robo-double get the better of her.

"I think we should move back a bit," she said, tugging her parents off the dance floor. "Awful gets worse every time she hears this song. Angrier and meaner. She's probably in full 'destroy' mode by now."

"Oh yes, things are really hotting up on the dance floor," said the DJ. "Rock on, Family Orr!"

"Spreading fear throughout the nation,
Feel our robot rage…"

Audrey called over to the bar. "Have you got enough footage yet, Mr Stickler? Can we switch the music off now?"

"Mr Stickler? As in your headmaster?" Mr Orr shook his head in disbelief. "Is there anyone who

isn't on board this ship?"

"Yes, thank you, Audrey, that should do the trick," said Mr Stickler, leaving the safety of the bar to join them. "Once the authorities see this clip they'll *have* to listen to us. If you could turn off the music now please, Mr Michaelton," he added, "before things get out of hand."

"*...It's time for confrontation...*"

"I said turn it off," repeated the headmaster, pointing to the music deck with his trusty ruler. But the DJ's eyes were still fixed on Awful, his head bobbing along in time to the song.

"You see?" said Mrs Orr, turning back to the security guard. His round red face had gone very pale all of a sudden. "*Now* do you believe us?"

"W-what's happening to her?" he stammered as he edged away, slowly.

"*ROBOT RAGE!*" screeched Awful, her face a twisted grimace of hate. The song seemed to have sent her completely over the edge this time. She lunged for the guard, hauling him up in the air by his tie knot.

"Woah," said the DJ. "How much coffee did *she* drink this morning?!"

Mr Orr nodded to himself. "Yep. Pretty sure that's not my Audrey."

"*Time for robot rage…*"

Mr Stickler pressed 'record' again as Awful began spinning the man round and round over her head, like a lasso.

"Do something," Mr Orr told his wife. "Make her stop."

"Do—something," echoed the security guard, as he circled the ceiling. "Make—her—stop!"

"TURN OFF THE MUSIC!" yelled Audrey but the DJ took no notice.

"Right, you trumped-up toaster on legs," said Mrs Orr, putting on her you're-in-big-trouble-now face. "Stop spinning that security guard or face the full force of my lamination!" She pulled a large red 'PØLSE (SAUSAGE)' sign out of her handbag and aimed it, sideways, like a killer frisbee.

Go Mum! thought Audrey. A laminated sign might not be the best weapon in the world, but the look of steely determination mixed with Mum-rage on Mrs Orr's face was enough to scare anyone.

"One..." Mrs Orr said, in her best telling-off voice.

"Hurry," begged the security guard.

"Two…" Mrs Orr's eyes narrowed.

"Thr—"

"Fine," agreed Awful. She let go of the guard's tie and he flew across the dance floor, screaming as he went. "This isn't over yet though. TIME FOR REVOLUTION!" Awful yelled, kicking down the DJ's platform with a flip-flopped foot before bounding out of the room, tossing chairs and tables over her shoulder as she went.

"No. That's definitely not *my* Audrey," said Mr Orr. "A father can always tell."

24

Release the Belly Button

"Look after the security guard," yelled Mr Stickler, waving his ruler at the dazed-looking DJ. "And get him to send for reinforcements."

He headed for the door, with his dressing-gowned *Bad Grandad* sidekick racing along beside him. "*'Behold my fishing rod of fury,'*" they yelled in unison. "*'I'm gonna get me a Catch of the Day!'*" The Orrs were a few steps behind.

"I should have toe-blasted her while I had the chance," said Mr Orr, limping along as fast as he could.

"I should have seen through her dirty robot lies and tricks," said Mrs Orr.

"I should never have said 'yes' to a techno-twin

in the first place," said Audrey. "It's all my fault."

The party rounded the corner to the main staircase and ground to a halt.

"Which way now?" said Grandad. "Did anyone see where she went?"

"Somewhere with lots of food, I expect," said Audrey. "She always gets hungry when she hears that song. And I mean *really* hungry. It's worse every time."

"To the restaurant!" yelled Grandad and Mr Stickler.

"Excellent," said Mr Orr, rubbing his hands together. "Nothing like chasing after a fake robot daughter for working up an appetite, is there?"

His limp seemed to disappear after that. As they neared the main restaurant, with its floor-to-ceiling mirrored wall and fancy chandeliers, he was a good few feet in front of everyone else. "Ooh, looks like lobster on the lunch menu today. Delicious!"

"Forget about your stomach for one minute, Pooh-pooh. We're here to find the robot."

"There she is!" yelled Mr Orr, pointing to the

back of the room.

Audrey squinted through the sea of curious faces—the place was surprisingly full for such an early sitting—to see her own face squinting back at her.

"No, Dad, that's just me in the mirror."

"Perhaps she went to a different restaurant?" suggested Mrs Orr.

"We'll soon find out," said Mr Stickler, rapping his ruler on the nearest table. "Quieten down now please everyone. Yes, that means you lot at the back as well. Good morning, passengers."

"Good morning, Mr Stickler," Audrey chanted back, on autopilot.

"We're looking for a girl exactly like this." He pointed at Audrey. "Did anyone see her come in?"

"You mean that big fat one coming out of the ladies' toilets over there?" piped up a heavily lipsticked lady in a pearl necklace. She pointed to Mr Stickler's left. "The one with the glowing red eyes and the torn-off tap in her hand?"

"I wouldn't say she was fat..." Audrey began.

She turned to where the lady was pointing, just in time to see an enormous-stomached Awful wielding a torn-off sink tap like a shotput. The robot drew back her arm with an angry grunt and hurled it, spinning through the air, towards her human twin's head.

Audrey flung herself sideways and the tap embedded itself in the wall behind her. "Y-yes," she stammered, her whole body jangling with shock. "P-perhaps she has put on a bit of weight." The robot's t-shirt was riding up high above her belly button now, only it wasn't a belly button anymore. It was more like a tube, telescoping out the middle of her stomach. "I'd forget about lunch if I were you," Audrey told Pearl Lady. "Get out of here while you still can."

"You heard her!" shouted Awful, aiming her weird tummy tube at the lady's table. *Psshhhhhhhhheewww!* A fierce stream of water came blasting out at top speed, knocking glasses and plates crashing off the table and sending the central flower arrangement shooting across the room. Pearl

Lady started screaming. And then everyone else seemed to join in, throwing back their chairs and falling over each other in their rush to get away.

"Watch out!" *Crash!* Someone caught the edge of their tablecloth as they got up, sending another shower of food and crockery flying off across the room after them.

"She's crazy!"

Psshhhhhhhhheewww! Smash! Crash!

"Aaaarrrggghhhh! Let's get out of here!"

"I stole your idea about the belly button water pistol," Awful told Grandad, her mouth twisting up at the edges at the sight of so much chaos. You couldn't really call it a smile though. "What do you think?"

"What do *I* think? I think enough's enough," said Grandad bravely. "The game's over, Awful. Ship security's already on its way. Why don't you give yourself up now?"

"Because it's time for REVOLUTION!" she roared, letting rip with another belly button burst of water. "Release the ROBOT RAGE!" She stopped off to cram a couple of half-eaten lobster dishes into her mouth. And then a few more from the next table.

Entire bread baskets of rolls disappeared down her throat as she raced round the room, blasting and eating… a bit more blasting… a bit more eating.

"LOB LIB THW WOBOT WEBOULTION!" she shouted, spraying the remaining diners with showers of crumbs as they headed for the door.

"What was that last bit, Pooh-pooh? I can't understand a word she's saying with her mouth full."

But Mr Orr was barely listening. He was too busy staring at Awful in slack-jawed amazement. "Wow! She *really* knows how to pack the free food in. Perhaps we *are* related after all."

"HOLD IT RIGHT THERE! NOBODY MOVE," came a loud voice from the restaurant doorway. It was the ship's captain. Ten of his biggest, burliest crew members advanced into the room behind him, followed by DJ Mike 'The Music' Michaelton.

"Woah, this place is well and truly *trashed*," said Mike. "You Orrs *really* know how to party."

Thank goodness, thought Audrey, still shaking from her close brush with a tearaway tap. She felt much better now that the captain was here though. *It's all over. Everything's going to be alright.*

"The police are on their way," the captain told Awful. He seemed to think it was all over too. "So why don't you give yourself up quietly and calmly?"

"Yeah?" Awful's lip curled into a sneer. "And why don't you stick your captain's cap up your big fat captain's—"

"That's enough, young lady," cut in Mr Stickler, shaking his ruler at her. "We don't tolerate that sort of behaviour at school and we won't tolerate it here either."

Awful glared back at him. It was a fizzing red glare, pulsing with anger and hatred, and Audrey felt her confidence slipping away again.

Nobody moved for what felt like forever. They were all watching and waiting to see what happened next. Which turned out to be Awful lunging towards Grandad with a tiger-like snarl and grabbing him by the neck of his dressing gown.

"Dad!" screamed Mrs Orr.

"Grandad!" Audrey could hardly bear to look. *Don't hurt him. Please don't hurt him.*

"Listen up, you stupid little humans," said Awful. "If anyone so much as *tries* to arrest me, you can kiss the old man goodbye. Stand back the lot of you."

Everyone took three steps back.

"Er… a bit less of the *old* if you don't mind," said Grandad, trying to lighten the atmosphere with a joke like always. But his face was deathly pale and Audrey could see his knees trembling under his dressing gown. No one was laughing.

"And then I want a helicopter out of here, to join my robot brothers and sisters in the revolution," Awful went on. "And as much food as I can carry. Otherwise the old man gets it."

"No," said Audrey. It was a shaky, half-whispered kind of 'no' but it was still a 'no'.

"What do you mean, 'no'?"

Audrey took a deep breath, summoning up her last few drops of courage. She couldn't let anything happen to Grandad. She *wouldn't* let anything happen to him. "I *mean*, let him go." She inched forwards, one terrified step at a time. "*I'm* the one who started all this. You should take me instead."

"No, pet," said Grandad. "You stay back there where it's safe. I've got this one covered."

"You heard him, Audrey," agreed Mrs Orr, stumbling past her daughter towards the robot. "Stay with your father. *I'll* take Grandad's place."

"No, Kat," said Mr Orr, hurrying after her. "I'll go."

"That's enough. The old man stays with me," said Awful, blasting Audrey's parents off their feet with super-strong bursts of belly button water. They landed in a jumbled wet heap like a pair of soggy ragdolls and didn't get up again. She must have knocked them out. "But you're quite right, Audrey," she went on, as if nothing had happened. "This *is* all your fault. Which is why I want you up against the wall over there. I think it's time to try out my *other* new modification and see if we can't hurry up that helicopter a bit." She grinned her horrible lopsided grin. "Just a quick zap to show everyone I mean business."

"A z-zap? What do you mean?"

"Why's she doing this anyway?" whispered DJ Mike. "Is she still upset about the dead goldfish or something?"

"Oh, you're going to love my new zapper," said Awful. "Like a real life Orz Um! Hurry up now. Get back against the wall or it's 'bye-bye Grandad Gulliver'."

It was a walk of ten or so metres to the big mirrored wall at the back of the restaurant but it felt more like a marathon. It took every ounce of bravery Audrey possessed to force one shaking foot in front of the other. But she did it. What choice did she have? Her parents were still slumped unconscious on the floor, thanks to *her* terrible twin. She couldn't let Awful hurt Grandad too.

"P-p-please," she stammered, as she shrunk back against the shiny surface of the mirror. "C-c-can't we just go back to how things were? S-start again?"

"No, Audrey," shouted Grandad, struggling, pale-faced, against the robot's steely grip. "Get away from there. I don't care what she does to me, as long as you're safe. The same goes for your mum and dad. They'd sacrifice themselves for you in a heartbeat."

Audrey nodded, silent tears slipping down her cheeks as she stood there, shaking. It was true. She knew it was. But there was no going back now. One way or another she had to see this thing through to the end. *It's not over 'til it's over*, she told herself. Orz Um had got out of tighter spots than this before...

"S-so how does this zapping work exactly?" she said. "Have you got a laser eye as well now?"

"Right first time!" said Awful. "Pretty exciting eh? It was so easy too! A couple of visits to the on-board beauty parlour and optician's to 'borrow' some spot-zapping lasers and super-strong lenses and here we are. I can't wait to see if it works..."

So she hadn't actually tried it yet! Maybe there was still a chance Audrey would make it out of this alive.

"And who better to test it on than Little Miss

Lazy Eye herself? Yes, that's right, ladies and gentlemen, the one and only Audrey Orr!" Awful let out a strange mechanical laugh as she peeled off her eye patch to reveal a super-thick magnifying lens fitted into her glasses. "And to think I wanted to swap places with *you*. To become *you*. You're a joke, Audrey, standing there, all shivering and pathetic like a coward."

No, thought Audrey, gritting her teeth together to keep them from chattering. *I might be shaking with fright, but that doesn't make me a coward. And for your information it's not a* lazy *eye, it's a* learning-to-see-better *eye. So there.* The prospect of being zapped to smoking nothingness by an evil robot put everything into perspective, somehow. So what if people laughed at her eye patch? They were the ones with the problem, not her. But Awful was right about one thing: *I* am *the one and only Audrey Orr*, she told herself, *and I'm not going down without a fight.*

"Okay," she said out loud, as a sudden burst of inspiration hit her. "You win. I should have switched you off when I had the chance. I should have pressed that little button behind your ear the professor told us about…" It was a bluff of course—Audrey didn't have a clue where her twin's off switch was—but it worked.

"It's not behind my ear, you moron. It's up my nose. And if you'd bothered to read the professor's instruction manual when he first gave it to you, you'd have realised that!"

True. They could have saved themselves a *lot* of bother if they'd known that earlier. *But at least we know now,* thought Audrey, with a fresh flutter of hope.

Come on, Grandad, we can do this. She held her breath as his hand crept up towards the robot's face. Nearly there. *That's it, right up her nostril.*

"But you didn't, did you?" said Awful, slapping Grandad's hand away with a noisy *thwack* and taking the last of Audrey's hope with it. "Because you're a lazy little human and I'm an unstoppable machine. Say goodbye to your lazy little human friends now, Audrey. It's time to split."

Mrs Orr stirred, moaning softly where she lay. "Audrey. My Audrey…"

"One…" said Awful, pushing her reinforced glasses up her nose and taking aim at Audrey's head.

Yes, time to split, Audrey thought numbly, replaying the robot's final taunt in her mind. That was her *life* she was talking about. How could Awful be so cold-blooded and casual about it?

"Two…"

Time to split… Audrey said her last mental goodbyes to her family: to Mum—her crazy, laminating, laugh-a-minute mum; to her funny, fungal-footed dad, with his terrible singing and bottomless belly; to her beloved Grandad—*oh Grandad, I'm so sorry I dragged you into this*. She even said a final farewell to Mr Stickler. He'd turned out to be pretty cool for a headmaster in the end.

"Three!"

A red beam of light shot across the restaurant at laser speed.

25

Nose-picking for Beginners

But just *before* the count of three Audrey did something she'd never done before. The splits. And she had Awful to thank for the idea. Her right leg went one way and her left leg went the other, while the laser beam shot clean over her head. *ZAP!* It bounced off the mirror and headed straight back to Awful in the mere blink of an eye. Even with her lightning quick robot reflexes, she didn't manage to duck in time.

Ssszzzzsssiiizzzle. There was a loud pop, a horrid smell like frying plastic, and then the top of her head burst open in a spray of hidden wires and complicated-looking electronic things that only a professor of robot engineering would recognise.

"What's… happening… to… me?" Awful gasped, staggering sideways as she released her grip on Grandad's neck.

"Quick," yelled Audrey. "Switch her off!"

Grandad didn't need telling twice. He cocked his index finger like a gun and rammed it straight up the robot's nose. "Take that you monstrous machine!"

"Get… off… me… old… man," Awful wheezed, the red of her eyes fading to a milky white nothing. But she wasn't down yet.

"And the other nostril," Audrey called, trying, and failing, to push herself back onto her feet.

"That's quite enough of the 'old man' stuff," said Grandad, some of the colour coming back to his cheeks as he rammed his finger up the robot's nose a second time.

"You tell her!" Mr Stickler cheered, waving his ruler around in excitement.

"Get… off… mwuuuuurrrrrrggggggghhhhh…" Awful's broken head flopped forwards on her neck and her knees buckled underneath her. She hit the ground with a thump.

"What was that?" said Mr Orr, coming round with a start. "Did someone mention lunch?"

"Audrey," moaned Mrs Orr groggily. "Where's my Audrey?"

"I'm here, Mum," she called. "I'd come and help you up, only I'm a bit stuck. Doing the splits is hard enough—*undoing* them seems pretty impossible."

"Here, let me help," said Mr Stickler, rushing to Audrey's aid, while Grandad and DJ Mike attended to her parents.

"That was some groovy show your daughter put on there," said Mike. "*Zap, zap, pow!*"

"It certainly was," agreed the headmaster. "Are you alright, Audrey?"

"I think so." She was still in one piece—that was the main thing—even if it *felt* like someone had sliced her down the middle. *Now I know why they call them the splits.* "It's finally over, isn't it?" she double-checked, sneaking another glance at Awful. The robot hadn't moved.

"It is for *her*," said Mr Stickler, following

Audrey's gaze. "And thanks to you, we know how to turn off the other rogue robots too." He shot her an embarrassed smile. "Of course, I'd have known that already if I'd bothered to read *my* copy of the manual before I left. I guess headmasters are just as lazy as everyone else."

"Audrey!" called Mrs Orr. "Thank goodness! Oh, my brave clever girl. You did it!"

Yes, thought Audrey, feeling a small swell of pride as she hobbled over to her parents. *I did it. I took on a crazy killer robot and I won!* Maybe she was more like Orz Um than she realised.

"Yo, groovy group hug," observed DJ Mike, trying to wriggle his way into their family reunion. Mrs Orr pushed him back with a firm elbow—she only had cuddles for Audrey and her husband. Cuddles so warm and squeezy—if a little on the water-blasted wet side—that Audrey's legs finally stopped trembling and the wild hammering in her ribcage slowed to a soft, steady beat. That's when she knew it was really, truly over. She was finally back where she belonged—the one and only Audrey

Orr. Then Mr Orr hugged a nearby bowl of bread rolls while Audrey hugged Grandad and Mr Stickler hugged DJ Mike. It was like one big hug-fest. And then the captain, who'd somehow managed to avoid hugging anyone, herded them all over to one of the abandoned tables, to wait for the ship's doctor to come and check them out.

Audrey closed her eyes against the ruins of the restaurant and let the relief seep through her body like a warm cup of hot chocolate, with double powder and extra drops of vanilla. She was dimly aware of things happening around her—of the police coming to take away Awful's crumpled shell; of a small army of restaurant staff sweeping up the broken glass and clearing the tables; of Mr Orr wrestling another basket of bread rolls back off a waiter—but she was happy to let it all wash over her as she sat there, smiling to herself. Everything was going to be alright now.

And it was. The ship's doctor recommended rest and relaxation for Audrey and a dry change of clothes for her parents, but declared all three of them perfectly fit and healthy. If anything, being knocked unconscious had given Mr Orr even *more* of an appetite than usual, judging by the number of chewed lobster tails piling up in the middle of the table. Grandad hadn't been quite so lucky—his fingers were still sore and swollen where Awful had thwacked him—but the doctor assured him that nothing was broken and he'd be back knitting again in no time.

"Thank goodness for that," he said. "I thought I might make us some matching robot jumpers to remember our adventures by."

As if we could ever forget, thought Audrey, although she was pleased to see him back to his old smiling self.

"It's been a wild few days, eh?" he said, chuckling to himself. "And I reckon you gave Orz Um a good run for her money with that splits trick of yours… oops, sorry pet, I forgot…" He put his hand over his mouth, realising his mistake.

"It's alright, Grandad. Orz Um's not a secret anymore. I'd like Mum and Dad to read my comics too."

Her parents beamed.

"I could help you with the drawings if you want," offered Mr Orr, picking his teeth with a stray lobster leg. "I'm a dab hand at stick men."

Mr Stickler strode over to their table before Audrey had a chance to answer. "I'm glad you're all still here." He smiled a rare headmasterly smile. "I wanted to say goodbye before I left for the airport."

"What?" said Audrey. "You're leaving?" She found she didn't even have to fake polite disappointment. She was genuinely sorry to see him go. "But what about the rest of the cruise?"

"I need to get straight back to Ivy Ridge," he said, "and make sure *my* robo-double gets switched off. Then maybe I can see about getting the school reopened. And there's Professor Droyde, of course. Someone needs to check on him too. Goodness knows what that Robot Rage song will have done to his precious P2. Don't worry," he added, seeing the fresh look of alarm on Audrey's face. "The captain's already been in touch with the British police to give them the heads up. And he's forwarded on that footage I took of Awful up in the Dance Bar so they know what they're dealing with. I'm sure they've got the whole situation under control but I won't be able to relax until I see for myself." He laughed, tapping his bandaged leg with his ruler. "Speaking of relaxing, my knee boils haven't hurt at all today. Perhaps what I needed was *more* stress, not less!"

"Then I suppose that's the end of my holiday too," said Audrey, "if you're reopening the school." *And I* still *didn't get to try the Soft-Scoop-2000.*

"I should hope not." Mr Stickler winked. "Not after such a nasty bout of *robotitus*. A full week's recovery I'd have thought, just to make sure you're not contagious."

Audrey let out a squeal of excitement. "Thank you, sir. I promise I'll learn as much as I can while we're away."

"I'll make sure of it," said Mrs Orr, as the headmaster handed her back the confiscated language cards. "*Tusen takk*, Mr Stickler. You're a star."

"Maybe we could fly back together, Archie," suggested Grandad. "It'd be nice to have a bit of company."

"Ah, no. I'm afraid not," said Mr Stickler. "Sorry."

"Oh, okay." Grandad's face fell. "Fair enough."

"Because I've just had another word with the captain now," went on the headmaster, "and he's agreed to let you take my place on the cruise. Given the exceptional circumstances."

"Really?" said Grandad. His eyes lit up. "That's incredibly generous of you, Archie."

"Not at all. You'll be doing me a favour," said Mr Stickler. "I'd hate for such a lovely holiday to go to waste. I'll leave you to talk it over with your family while I go and pack."

"We'd love you to stay, Dad," said Mrs Orr, looking pained. "Of course we would. But what about Mr Windybags? He'll be fading away by the time we get back."

"Spoiled rotten more like," said Grandad. "I left him with my old ladies at the care home, feeding him up on leftover cooked breakfasts. Trumping like a trooper he was when I last saw him."

"Well I hope you warned them about their slippers." Mr Orr reached over to the next table for another uneaten lobster. "You know what he's like—eyes bigger than his belly."

"Please say you'll stay, Grandad," begged Audrey. "Please, please, please. It'll be the best holiday ever."

26

Soft-Scoop-2000

"*There* you are," said Audrey, when Grandad joined them on the sun deck a couple of days later, clutching a tropical fruit smoothie. "I was starting to worry something had happened to you."

"*I* was more worried about the lack of fizzy rainbow sherbet drops," said Mr Orr, pointing to the Soft-Scoop-2000. "Someone said they were running dangerously low."

"That still leaves fifty-one other toppings to choose between," his wife pointed out. "I'm sure you'll manage."

"What do you mean 'choose between'? I want *all* of them. I've waited all holiday for this. I'll be having a twenty-scoop mega-cone with every topping going."

Audrey rolled her eyes at Grandad and giggled. "You should have seen him at the Norwegian cheese and chocolate tasting earlier... it's a wonder he can still walk!"

"Yes, I'm sorry I missed that," said Grandad. "But I couldn't turn down *The Scandinavian Queen's* famous knitting workshop, could I? I've been itching to pick up my needles again now the swelling's gone down in my fingers. And then, just as I was leaving, I got a message from the captain saying they had Archie on the ship's phone. That's why I'm so late. Well, that and a quick stop at the smoothie bar. Knitting workshops are thirsty work you know."

"You've been talking to Mr Stickler? What did he say? Is Professor Droyde okay? And what about the school? What happened when the police got there?"

"Hold your horses!" Grandad laughed. "One question at a time." He lowered himself down onto the sun lounger Audrey had saved for him and took a long slurp of his smoothie. "Professor Droyde's absolutely fine," he reassured her. "P2 did go a bit nuts for a while there, as you know, but it turns out he's not very good at tying people up. The professor was able to wriggle out of his ropes before any real damage was done and switch him back off. He must have had a lot of explaining to do to the police afterwards, but from what Archie said it doesn't sound like they'll be pressing charges. Not now all the robo-doubles are accounted for. I guess the professor would argue it was that song that did the real damage."

"*All* the robots, did you say? Including Mr Stickler's? Does that mean he'll be able to reopen the school?"

Grandad nodded. "He will now Professor Droyde's installing a new computing system to make up for the smashed machines. The governors couldn't really say no to that."

"Phew, that's good," said Audrey, realising she actually meant it. This time last week she couldn't wait to get away from school, but that was the *old* Audrey Orr. The one who let a silly little thing like an eye patch get between her and the chance to make new friends. Who cared if the little kids pointed at her in the lunch queue? They were too young to know any better. And so what if a handful of silly boys made pirate jokes behind her back? Audrey had tackled *far* worse problems than that. *Yes, things are going to be different when I get home*, she promised herself. It was time to stop hiding and start living.

"Wait a minute," she said, as another thought struck her. "Are you sure these new computers of Professor Droyde's are safe? What if *they* get infected with robot rage too?"

Grandad patted her arm. "Of course they'll be safe, pet. That Terence and the Machines song only affects techno-twins and they've all been taken care of. Now, are we going to try out this Soft-Scoop-2000 or not?"

"Finally!" Mr Orr was already off, hurdling over sleeping sunbathers in his rush to get to the front of the queue.

"I'll take that as a 'yes'," said Grandad.

"Wel-come," chanted a metallic lady's voice, as Mr Orr pressed the start button on the green touch screen. A list of available flavours and toppings flashed up, with allergy advice beside each one. "What ice cream com-bin-a-tion would you like to-day?"

Mr Orr didn't even need to think about it. "I'll have the biggest cone you've got, please, with vanilla, strawberry, chocolate, raspberry ripple, pistachio, rum and raisin, ginger crunch…"

"Sorry," said Mrs Orr, as another family joined the queue behind them. "You might have a bit of a wait."

"Delicious," said Audrey, finishing off her mint-choc-chip mega-cone with chocolate raisin sprinkles.

"Delicious," agreed Grandad. "This really is the best holiday ever. Sun, sea and soft-scoop ice cream on tap. What more could anyone ask for?"

"Some fizzy rainbow sherbet drops might have been nice," said Mr Orr grumpily, rubbing at the melted mess of flavours dripping down his shirt. "Only joking," he added, breaking into a grin. "You're right, this *is* the best holiday ever. Bit of a rocky start, what with one thing and another, but that's all behind us now. Three cheers for Kat for winning such a fabulous pr—"

The rest of the sentence died away to nothing as a sunburnt man in Bermuda shorts came strolling past clutching a portable radio. A portable radio playing a horribly familiar song:

"*...Let's smash the institution*
With our robot rage,
Spreading fear throughout the nation,
Feel our robot rage,
It's time for confrontation,
Time for robot rage..."

"Huh," said Mrs Orr, breaking the long silence that followed. "I never did like that tune. Don't worry though, sweetheart," she added, leaning over to squeeze Audrey's hand. "It can't do any more harm. We're safe now."

"Hmm," said Audrey, looking over at the Soft-Scoop-2000's glowing red screen. "I hope you're right."